T0072521

SILVERBACK

JANOESHA HARBOUR Book 3

M C Williams

BALBOA.PRESS
A DIVISION OF HAY HOUSE

Balboa Press books may be ordered through booksellers or by contacting:

Balboa Press
A Division of Hay House
1663 Liberty Drive
Bloomington, IN 47403
www.balboapress.com
844-682-1282

Because of the dynamic nature of the Internet, any web addresses or
links contained in this book may have changed since publication and
may no longer be valid. The views expressed in this work are solely those
of the author and do not necessarily reflect the views of the publisher,
and the publisher hereby disclaims any responsibility for them.

The author of this book does not dispense medical advice or prescribe the use
of any technique as a form of treatment for physical, emotional, or medical
problems without the advice of a physician, either directly or indirectly. The
intent of the author is only to offer information of a general nature to help
you in your quest for emotional and spiritual well-being. In the event you use
any of the information in this book for yourself, which is your constitutional
right, the author and the publisher assume no responsibility for your actions.

Any people depicted in stock imagery provided by Getty Images are
models, and such images are being used for illustrative purposes only.
Certain stock imagery © Getty Images.

Print information available on the last page.

ISBN: 978-1-9822-5335-6 (sc)
ISBN: 978-1-9822-5336-3 (e)

Balboa Press rev. date: 09/08/2020

CONTENTS

MAIN CHARACTERS

1. Moses Uatobuu
2. Stacey Lane
3. Neilson Gainer
4. General Banes
5. Aaron Fentcal
6. Audrey Boyner
7. Sedrick Tate
8. Remni Claus
9. Gwen Stevens
10. Maureen Robertson
11. Frank Allister
12. Shelby Chamberlain
13. Ruth Onomauwae
14. Ray Gatlain
15. Jessepi Montoya
16. Kelso Ramirez
17. Robert Teal
18. Janet Jacobson
19. Bruno Ellk
20. Lieutenant Janes
21. Greg Olson
22. Sterling Myers
23. Walt Buyer
24. Lieutenant Gormann

North Tamerra The Rockhound subdivision
May 3rd, 2020

The Rockhound subdivision is just thirty minutes north of downtown Tamerra by car. It's a project put together by the city, city officials signed a contract with JHarbour Corp to extend Tamerra's suburb to the north. JHarbour Corp is a building that's located in downtown Tamerra it specialize in Regional Infrastructure, they built most of the roads and buildings in the Edward Region. The contract stated that each party agreed upon a three year(s) Building

Agreement and that it was okay for JHarbour Corp to hire Building Contractors. The contract was for a subdivision of raised-bungalows to be built, the starting date of construction would be the 28thof April 2020, it was do to the population growth in Tamerra.

Moses was working at the Rockhound subdivision laying brick, he was with a contractor from south Tamerra named ENCO Craftmen Inc they are a fourteen man crew of Bricklayers and Cement-finishers. Moses was on a lunch break, he had just completed the entrance to the Rockhound subdivision. The entrance was two red-brick walls on both sides of the road that lead into the subdivision, both walls had a tunneled walkway so a sidewalk can go through, the walls were shaped like a upside down ax blade with the blade facing the road, they stood at twelve feet in height. Moses sat in his charcoal-gray 2015 Ford F-150 eating a roast beef sandwich on a kaiser, he had been living and working in Tamerra for a little over a year, he just sign onto an eight months contract with ENCO Craftmen. Moses cell-phone that was on the dashboard started ringing, from the call display feature he could see that it was Stacey Lane, he answered it, she was calling to see if he wanted to come by her place for dinner. How could he say no to Stacey Lane "sure I'll be finished around six" he replied and she hung up on her end.

Moses put the phone back on the dashboard and took a Blue Toucan out of his truck's glove-compartment, he twist the cap off the bottle and started drinking.

Stacey Lane is a thirty year old rich girl from Elm's Green, she is the daughter of Neil (The Steel) Lane a famous Laamb Wrestler from the 1970's and 80's, he was a five time world-champion. Stacey works at TJNX News as a journalist she studied journalism at the University Of Janoesha Harbour in Alan's Landing and graduated with honors. Stacey found out about an opening at TJNX News at a job fair in the university, she faxed them her cover-letter and resume, a week later they called her for an interview and two weeks after that she was hired on. Stacey packed up her things in Spirit's Cove and moved out to Tamerra.

Stacey was at her desk going over some paperwork, it was the end of the work-day for her at the newsroom she was just finishing up organizing her leads and tagging each video-drive she filled. The night before her and her camera-man named Sedrick snuck into The Space Lab. Stacey read about corruption going on there, they were secretively splicing primate and human DNA, Doctor Gainer a cellular biologist that works at The Space Lab explained at a press conference that the primate gene had something in it that slowed down the aging process in humans, so Stacey and Sedrick went over to The Space Lab late one night to collect evidence of the corruption, Stacey discovered a flash-drive on it was General Banes at a press conference speaking on the same topic of DNA the general also endorsed a check for $700,000 to The Space Lab towards the primate program. Stacey put the flash-drive in her blue-suede purse. Now today she was finishing up for the day and during dinner this evening she'll show Moses the flash-drive maybe he'll know what to do with it "Stacey you wanna go to the bar for a couple" Sedrick asked her as he left his desk and headed for the door "I'm going to have to put a rain-check on that Sedrick" she replied "okay see you tomorrow" he said as he left through the door, not too long after she followed behind him.

It was 5:30pm and Moses was loading his tools in the bed of his pick-up truck, it had been a long day for him and all he wanted to do was go home and take a shower then get some rest before he had to meet up with Stacey. After he loaded all his tools in the pick-up Moses left, he drove along Route 12 that lead from the Rockhound subdivision and connected onto Route 55. Moses turned left onto Route 55, the drive on 55 was a pleasant one not much traffic until he got closer to the city then it was bumper to bumper traffic. The traffic didn't really faze Moses because his turn-off was coming up soon at Route 18. Moses lived in a two bedroom apartment on Route 18 just east of Route 55. He was living there rent free for eight months, ENCO Craftmen was paying for him to live there, if he wanted to stay there beyond the eight months he would have to pay the rent out of his own pocket. The building has four floors each apartment has a balcony, Moses lived on the top floor. When Moses got home he took a shower and then put on a pair of shorts and a clean t-shirt, he heated up some left over chicken in the microwave-oven he had in the fridge from the night before. Moses sat on the couch in the living room in front of the TV eating his chicken and watching the news until he fell a sleep.

The Space Laboratory started out as a study-building for fossil research and a museum in the day time, but throughout the years it has evolved into the central-station of Janoesha Harbour's wild life research with scientist from all over the world studying and working out of its research facilities. The Space Laboratory or 'Space Lab' as the locals like to call it is located just north of the city of Tamerra it sits just southwest of the foothills from the Turynfoymus Mountain Range. Its backyard houses different species of animals. The building is built of white concrete that frame is steel re-bar its back end is built like a dome the front is a half-saddle or a check mark, the front is made of polished-steel. The Space Lab was built back on February 7th 1869 on behalf of a Oscar Mumbaywae Saulmon a professor of medicine that lived on the island.

Neilson Gainer is a sixty-three year old cellular biologist that works at the Space Lab he's with a team of scientist that are working on the primate program. He just entered into his condominium closing the door behind him and sitting around the dining room table, the window in the dining room overlooked the city of Tamerra. Neilson sat there reading the newspaper mentally drained from a long day at work, its a wonder he was able to read the paper. Neilson got to his feet went over to the fridge and poured himself a glass of scotch whiskey, he took two swigs just to calm his nerves. Neilson Gainer was born on May 4th 1957 in Brookshore, he spent the first fourteen years of his life in Brookshore and then moved with his parents to Alan's Landing when his dad got a job at the Plymouth dealership on Shore Street. Neilson's father was born in Luxor, Egypt and his mother is from Toulouse, France, his parents met on Janoesha Harbour in 1950. Neilson has a older sister born in 1954, she's a retired school teacher that lives in Amaryllis Jaiz. Neilson's appearance is quite cryptic when first meeting him, he stands at six feet tall and weighs a 165 pounds, his upper back is slightly hunched over, his beak-like nose and high cheek-bones makes him look like a mad scientist when he wears his glasses.

Moses woke up to the sound of a Brown booby squawking on his balcony, after a while the large bird flew away, he rubbed the sleep out of his eyes as he stretched his body out of slumber. Moses got to his feet and headed for the bedroom to get dress, he checked for any messages on his phone that was on the coffee table in the living room, there was one, it was from Stacey saying that she wanted to check out the new Cuddle Friendly's in town it just opened up a week ago. Moses replied 'okay' to her message and got dressed. After Moses finished brushing his teeth he grabbed his keys and his wallet off the bed and headed out, Moses took the staircase instead of the elevator, when he got to street-level he went through a back door that lead into the underground parking which is actually street-level parking, he hopped into his pick-up truck. He sat in his truck thinking about Stacey's message "Cuddle Friendly's" he says to himself 'it's going to be a steak and ribs night, gonna have to rob a bank to pay for this bill' Moses thought as he chuckled to himself. Moses started up the pick-up and backed out onto Route 18 and headed east to pick up Stacey.

Stacey met up with Moses out front of her condo on Route 22 & 53. She wore a ethnic sleeveless beach neck floral summer dress with a pair of cross band wedge sandals on her feet, her hair was done up in braids. Moses pulled into the vacant parking spot in front of her, she was on her phone playing Solitaire when he pulled in an hadn't noticed him until he beeped his horn and waved at her. Stacey saw Moses waving at her, she put her phone back in her purse and headed over to his truck, when she got there she opened up the passenger side door and hopped in. As Stacey shuffled about to get comfortable in the seat Moses was admiring her soft brown legs, he put his hand on her thigh as she fixed her hair "you look beautiful sweets" he told her as he gently squeezed her thigh, she gasped in delight and let out a giggle "after dinner you'll get your dessert" she told Moses, Moses gave her a smile as she closed the door and he turned out of the parking spot he was in and headed west on Route 22 to the beach. The restaurant was located at Route 55 & 26 on the same side as AquaHorn Beach. Moses knew the route that Stacey loved he's driven it with her before, she loved driving on the 55 especially at night the water seemed tranquil to her like a masterpiece painting that was put there to remind us of the beauty of nature's existence. The way Moses seen it was from 22 down the 55 to 26 is about a ten minute drive, not bad especially when your passenger looks like Stacey Lane, Moses smiled to himself and gave Stacey a hug with his free hand "thanks for driving this way" she told him "I knew you would like it" he replied. Traffic had died down on Route 55 everyone was settled in for the night, the yachts in the marina had their lights on and the hotels windows along the 55 were filled with lights. As they got closer to their destination Stacey could see that the beach was filled with people 'must be a concert going on' she thought to herself. Cuddle Friendly's was located at the south end of AquaHorn Beach unlike the original Cuddle Friendly's in Alan's Landing this one has a beach-front patio with a man-made waterfall and Tiki-bar. Moses pulled into the parking lot of Cuddle Friendly's, Cuddle Friendly's was built of powdered-blue marble and mahogany wood to Moses and Stacey it seemed spread out everything built on one level with its two door entrance and hat-check plus powder-room for the ladies, not to mention its huge patio. Moses back into a vacant parking spot "looks like it's fairly busy in there" Moses said to Stacey as he put the truck in park, Stacey looked over at the people going into Cuddle Friendly's "yeah maybe we'll even get a table right away" she replied. Moses opened his door and jumped out of the truck he went around to the passenger side and opened the door for Stacey, she motioned like she was about to jump out of the truck but Moses lifted her out and kicked the door shut, he was carrying her like they just gotten married. Stacey started giggling and laughing as Moses danced around while holding her in his arms "put me down Mo" she said to him "you crazy man" she added with a smile. Moses put her down and kissed her on the cheek, they held hands as they went to the restaurant's entrance. When they got to the entrance they could see that it wasn't too busy inside, they were greeted by a waitress as they entered inside "welcome to Cuddle Friendly's, is this for a party of two" she asked them with a smile "yes please" Stacey replied. The waitress escorted Moses and Stacey to a table out on the patio, it was a warm night so they didn't mind, she placed two menus on the table "can I get you anything to drink" she asked Moses and Stacey as they sat down around the table "yes a Blue Toucan for me and a double of Salu! on the rocks with a lemon twist for the lady" Moses replied, the waitress left to get there drinks. "You remembered my drink" Stacey said to Moses "I sure did love" he replied smiling at her, Stacey and Moses had been seeing each other for awhile some would even say it's a serious relationship, strange thing is though they never thought of living with each other. I guess there's a unspoken understanding between them knowing each others job an there demands. "It's nice in here" Moses said looking around "yeah my aunt Edith came here opening day" Stacey told Moses and continued "she said the first hundred people that came in ate for free" "is that Jake's mother" Moses asked her "yes" Stacey replied wondering what he meant by that "how's he doing" Moses inquired "he's still in Young Rangers, he recently receive the Silver Honey Badger Crest for his intelligence and ingenuity" she told Moses "that's excellent, how long now has he been in The Rangers" Moses said "it's been a little over two years but he likes it, his parents say he's planning on joining the services on his eighteenth birthday" Stacey replied "how old is he now" Moses asked "sixteen" Stacey answered "hmm" Moses said as he leaned back in his chair. The waitress returned with there drinks and placed them on the table "have you decided on what to eat" she asked them "give us a few more minutes" Moses replied "take your time" the waitress told him and left. "So young Jake Bower wants to be a soldier" Moses said "can we please stop talking about my family" Stacey asked Moses "okay we can change the topic" Moses replied as he held both her hands, he looked out at the water and then back at her "remember when we use to make love on the beach and go skinny-dipping late at night" he said while he caressed her hands. "I didn't mean we should talk about that" Stacey said with a shy schoolgirl look on her face "okay what's on your mind" Moses asked her "I have something to show you" she replied "what is it" Moses said intrigued "first I have to tell you that me and a camera-man from the news station snuck into the Space Lab last night" Stacey said "you did what" Moses reacted shock to hear that from her "I believe there's corruption going on at the Space Lab and now I have the proof, they're doing genial cloning there, they're working on slicing primate

DNA with human DNA" she explained to Moses "that's impossible it can't be done" Moses told her "yes because both DNA are similar they found away to combined them" she told Moses. "Even if that were true it would take a lot of money to get that done" Moses informed her "well that's what I was about to tell you, I took a flash-drive from there, on the flash-drive there's a video of General Banes endorsing a check for $700,000 towards the Primate Program that's what they call it" she told Moses "I don't think that was a wise decision to take the flash-drive, you don't know who these people are, you might have putting yourself into something you can't get out of" he explained to her "the flash-drive is my proof plus you know General Banes" Stacey said to Moses "yes I do, I can't believe he would be apart of something like this" Moses replied "we can watch it when we get back to your place" Stacey said as she gave Moses a smile. Moses knew what that smile meant (dessert was going to be served at home) "okay" he said smiling back at her.

The morning opened up with a sun-shower coming down over Tamerra, the rain had drenched the streets but they didn't stay wet for too long, the intense rays from the sun soon dried them up. At the Space Lab Neilson Gainer also referred to as Doctor Gainer was just starting his day at work, he was researching the differences in the primate cell structure and the human cell structure, he noted that the bond could be made from their nucleus the only obstacle is that the primate membrane is thicker than humans. Doctor Gainer had been working on this for three days, his assistant was a young lady that looked to be in her late twenties, she had on a white lab-coat with her hair done up in a bun. She came in the Cellular Research room where Doctor Gainer was "Doctor they've brought in the silver back gorillas" she informed Doctor Gainer "thank you Audrey" Doctor Gainer replied.

In one section of the Space Lab that they named The Farm was a large round room like a silo where the guards at the Space Lab and Janoesian soldiers were herding gorillas into. They had tagged them with a metal next-bracelet so the gorilla would stay on the property if a gorilla happens to breach the perimeter-fence the bracelet would trigger a silent-bomb therefore decapitating the animal.

Audrey stood there in the open doorway of the Cellular Research room "is there anything else" Doctor Gainer asked as he turned around from what he was doing to face her "yes the general is coming by this afternoon, apparently there was a security-breach in the building two nights ago and a flash-drive has gone missing from the computer room" she informed Doctor Gainer and left. Doctor Gainer was thankful to Audrey for relaying that message to him because most of the flash-drives and files in the computer room were top secret. This really worried Doctor Gainer so he got on the phone and called upstairs to the security-guards room, he told them to bring up recordings of all security-cameras from two nights ago and hold them until he comes by this afternoon.

Moses woke up the next day feeling groggy, he sat up in bed, yawning and stretched out his arms the warm breeze from outside blew through his open bedroom window billowing the silk-white curtains inward. He then realized by looking next to him that Stacey had spent the night 'yeah that's right the flash-drive, we must of watched it' he thought to himself as he took the covers from off his lap, he was naked and so was Stacey laying there next to him. Moses leaned back to see what time it was on his clock-radio, it was 8:15am, he had to be at work in forty-five minutes "time to get up" he said as he gave Stacey two slaps on her soft round bare bottom and slid out of bed. Stacey moaned and finally opened her eyes, Moses went to take a shower, Stacey still felt tired from the night before, she slowly rolled over and sat up in bed, at lease she got to show Moses the flash-drive 'what to do next' she thought to herself she initially decided to bring it to Public Announcement Corp (PAC) but what Moses was talking about last night gave her second thoughts.

Public Announcement Corp (PAC) is a investigative division of the federal government it is run by a team of investigators and crime-reporters. What they do is investigate all forms of white-collar crime and corruption, whether it's an individual, group, private business, contractor, franchise or government, they investigate and whatever they find they put out into the media. They're also known for excepting evidence from people that come into their building. There's a PAC building located in downtown Tamerra and there's another one in Brookshore those are their corporate buildings they have offices all over Janoesha Harbour.

After Moses and Stacey took a shower they got dress and left to go to work, Moses was going to drop off Stacey at the news station on his way to work, she had a change of clothes in her locker there. They made a pit-stop at a coffee shop to pick up breakfast to-go (two Egg McMuffin on a sesame bagel with a couple cans of orange-juice) and continued on. Stacey took the flash-drive out of her purse and handed it to Moses "here hold on to this it will be safe with you I'll pick it up later" she told him as she stuffed it in his pants pocket, Moses took it out and put it in his truck's glove-compartment. Moses pulled into the front lobby of the news station, Stacey opened up her side door "should I pick you up later" Moses asked her "yeah come by around six" she replied, they hugged each other and kissed "I really enjoyed last night" she told Moses as she caressed his muscular chest. After their temporary goodbyes Stacey got out of the truck and went into the news station.

Head security-guard Aaron Fentcal sat in the security room with two of his co-workers looking over the video-tapes from two nights ago "try to capture every second, the security-cameras work in time sections" Aaron told his co-workers. The two men that were there with him were computer analyst and they had knowledge on how to slow down the tape to show every section. Aaron studied closely as the men watched the tape in slow-mode, a few minutes went by and then they were able to see two figures entering the computer room a man and a women, the man was holding a camcorder in his hand, the lady looked familiar to Aaron but he just couldn't put his finger on where he's seen her before. "Freeze it right there" Aaron told the two men "blow it up and then clean up the pixelation" he instructed them as he got up out of his chair to get more coffee from the dispenser that was in the room.

Forensic Anthropologist Remni Claus was down in one of the research labs that was on the main floor of the Space Lab he was studying some bones the Janoesian Army found a few years back in the western region of the Turynfoymus Mountain Range. He cut one of the bones in cubes to extracted DNA from the marrow, as he was placing each cube into a clear plastic vile a security-guard knocked on his door. Remni stopped what he was doing and went over and opened the door "sorry to disturb you Doc they want to see you in the computer room in forty-five minutes" the guard informed him "thank you" Remni said. Remni Claus is a fifty-two year old anthropologist born August 12th 1967 in Brookshore, Janoesha Harbour, he's actually from Humblerock a suburb of Brookshore. His father was born in north Africa and came to Janoesha Harbour with his parents at the age of two. Remni's dad worked in the larimar and alexandrite mines for fifty-one years as a Mine Engineer that's how he met Remni's mom at a union social function, she's from Freiburg, Germany who worked as a Principal Resource Geologist with the International Mining Corporation. Remni's parents are now retired and still living in Brookshore, they've been married and together for fifty-two years. Remni got back to what he was doing, he finished putting the cubes in the viles, Remni was very curious to know why they wanted him in the computer room "hope there wasn't a fire" he said to himself.

In a research lab next to the one Remni was in Pathologist Gwen Stevens had on her table was a fully grown silver-back gorilla, it had died from some disease that caused its skin and muscles to rot. Gwen took some of the gorillas blood so she could run a series of tests on it. Gwen Stevens is a twenty-eight year old surgical pathologist, she grew up near AquaHorn Beach in the wealthy and prestigious Bluewinds neighborhood, she studied at the University of Janoesha Harbour in Alan's Landing. Gwen's parents are hydrologist at Sharesta Gardens, they test the water there for any foreign bacteria that might be harmful to ocean life, they've been working there twenty-five years now. Gwen has only been working at the Space Lab for two years that is why the guard didn't knock on her door, I guess she's not apart of the Primate Program. Gwen started washing her hands and getting ready to head out for lunch, a friend of her's told her about a sandwich place down the street that just opened up, she was planning on checking it out. Gwen took off her lab-coat and laid it across the back of a chair beside the table the gorilla was on, she grabbed her purse and headed out the door.

Moses had stopped working and was sitting in his truck enjoying his lunch-break, he was thinking about the flash-drive Stacey left with him, the whole memory of last night is coming back now, him and Stacey actually watched the flash-drive on his laptop and from what he saw was General Banes giving a check of $700,000 to the organizer of the Primate Program a Doctor Neilson Gainer a cellular biologist. Moses remembers that they mentioned little about what the Primate Program was about (being naive with the particulars) and he also remembers seeing way too many soldiers at that press conference as if the program is funded by the army and for the army "interesting" Moses said to himself as he held the flash-drive in his hand. Moses looked at the flash-drive in his hand 'I know someone at Base Laysan that might know more about this' Moses thought to himself as he continued to stare at the flash-drive. Moses put the flash-drive back in the glove-compartment and got on his cell-phone, he was calling Frank in Base Laysan, the phone rang a few times and then went to voice-mail "hey Frank how you doing it's Moses, can you give me a call back after five there's something I want to ask you" Moses left a message. Moses and Frank still kept in contact as a matter of fact Moses and Stacey was at his place for Christmas dinner last year when Karen got drunk and passed out in the bathtub, Moses chuckled to himself just thinking about that point in time.

General Banes convoy pulled up to the entrance gate of the Space Lab, the general was in a 2018 Cadillac XT5, the Cadillac drove up to the security-booth and stopped, its back passenger window opened. "Good afternoon General" the security-guard on duty said to General Banes "has everyone been informed of this meeting" General Banes asked the security-guard "yes sir they have" the security-guard replied and saluted the general. General Banes returned a salute as his convoy made its way to the front lobby of the Space Lab.

In the computer room everyone that was invited to the meeting was gathered there, there was Remni Claus, Neilson Gainer, Aaron Fentcal and Maureen Robertson a senior ethologist at the Space Lab, they were now waiting on General Banes the one that called this meeting. Aaron pulled a computer-disc out of his pants pocket "I think I know who broke in here two nights ago" he said as he held up the disc in his hand for everyone to see "who was it" Neilson asked him "here watch" Aaron told Neilson as he slipped the disc into one of the many computers in the room, everyone gathered around and watched. Aaron had cleaned up the pixelation of the video and slowed in down a bit, they seen two figures come into the computer room the male figure seems to be recording stuff and the female figure was rifling through desks and turning on computers like she was looking for something. They then seen her put a flash-drive in her purse, Aaron paused the video "an there you have it" he said to everyone "who was that" Maureen asked anyone that had the answer "more important how did they get pass security" Neilson added "I'm still looking into that sir" Aaron replied "I still would like to know who these people are" Maureen inquired as she point at the computer-screen "her name is Stacey Lane and she's a crime-journalist with TJNX News" a voice said behind them, they all turned around to see who it was, it was General Banes and two of his soldiers "how do you know that" Remni asked him "because I know her boyfriend" the general replied. General Banes walked over to the group of scientist "gentlemen and lady I believe we have the upper hand here and also a test-subject" the general told them with a smile "what do you mean" Neilson asked "my men went to retrieve the young journalist so not to worry all is good" General Banes assured everyone "who's the other person" Maureen inquired "that's her camera-man Sedrick Tate" the general replied.

Stacey was at her desk going over some paperwork, she just finished broadcasting the afternoon news. Stacey covered the investigative side of the news called Crime Beat, it focuses on crime in the city of Tamerra and the surrounding boroughs. Stacey was waiting for Sedrick to come back with the news-van so they could head out to the Emmlor's Pond neighborhood, there was a double murder there, a wife and husband were bounded and stabbed to death with their throats sliced. Stacey wanted to get there soon, apparently the bodies were discovered a half an hour ago she found out from a friend in the newsroom. Stacey's office was part of a four office cubical with disassembling walls dividing each office, a co-worker in the office in front of her told Stacey with a concerned look on her face that some men were here to see her, before she could turn around in her seat to go see who it was two soldiers came in her office and stood over her "Miss Lane you've been summoned by the Janoesian Government you need to come with us" one soldier said as they held her by the arms and escorted her outside to an a waiting vehicle. Stacey was confused in what was going on, at the outdoor lobby she was thrown in a black-van when she was inside a black cloth sack was put over her head so she couldn't see and her wrist were bounded behind her back with flex-cuffs. Stacey's body was pumping adrenaline as she cried and begged them not to kill her.

Sedrick went back to his place to grabbed a new lens he bought for his camera yesterday. He parked the news-van on the curb in front of the house he was renting, he wasn't going to be too long, he had forgotten the lens on the kitchen counter this morning when he left for work. Sedrick opened the front door to his house and went in, he went into the kitchen and got the lens, he put the lens-cap on and put it in his camera-bag he wore over his shoulder. Sedrick went to use the washroom he knew he wasn't going to have a chance to once he got back to the news station because him and Stacey was scheduled to be out in Emmlor's Pond. When he came out of the washroom after washing and drying his hands he smelt the faint sent of gas so he went back into the kitchen to check the stove, one of the knobs for the burners wasn't quite off so he turned it to the off position, right then the house blew-up. Out on the other side of the street in front of the house, right after the house blew-up a black-sedan sped away.

Frank was working as a mechanical engineer designing parts for tanks in a stockpile on Base Laysan, he was now Staff Sergeant Frank Allister. It was the end of the work day for Frank and he was heading home, on his way home he was listening to Moses message on his cell-phone that he had in a cradle mounted on the dashboard of his jeep 'it's always good to hear Moses voice' he thought to himself. Frank looked at his watch it was 5:15pm so he gave Moses a call, he had his number on speed-dial, the phone rang twice and Moses picked up "hello" Moses said as Frank put him on speaker-phone "how you doing Captain" Frank replied "hey Frank, not bad just on my way home" Moses said "how's Tamerra" Frank asked him "same old thing" Moses replied, Frank chuckled at Moses comment. "So whats up Mo" Frank asked "what do you know about a Primate Program General Banes is running" Moses replied "oh that, well I'm kept in the dark about that but what I do know is that the general is planning on building stronger soldiers through splicing DNA, only a selected bunch of soldiers are a part of the program it's very hush hush" Frank said "does the president know about this" Moses inquired "no but I believe someone in his cabinet has to know something" Frank replied "being that Banes is a four star general he would need permission from President Myers" Moses said "this has been in the planning-stage a few years now, I believe they're flying below the president's radar" Frank informed Moses. There was a thirty second pause of silence on the phone "how do I stop this from happening" Moses then asked "you don't" Frank replied "Stacey broke into the Space Lab and took a flash-drive, on the flash-drive is a press conference of General Banes endorsing $700,000 to the program" Moses informed Frank "where's the flash-drive now" Frank asked him "she left it with me" Moses replied "give it back Mo you don't won't to get involve with this" Frank told him. Frank pulled into his driveway and put the jeep in park, he took his phone out of it's cradle and turned it off speaker-phone "I gotta go Mo, please don't get tangled up in this, I'm telling you as a friend" Frank told Moses and then hung up the phone.

Moses hung up the phone after speaking with Frank, he tossed the phone on the passenger seat, he was on his way to pick up Stacey, he had a bit of time left so he decided on stopping off at a coffee shop to get something cold to drink. Moses pulled into the parking lot of the coffee shop and parked his truck, before he went in to order his drink he turned on the radio to find out the score of the Kelo-ball game that was played last night. Surfing through the channels his attention cot a broadcast from TJNX News, Janet Jacobson a journalist at the news station was reporting from the scene, apparently a house on Route 18 and 55 blew up, they said the body of twenty-seven year old Sedrick Tate a camera-man for TJNX news was pulled from the rubble, so far that was the only body they found. The cause of the explosion was undetermined, right now they were calling it a gas leek, Bomb Investigator Bruce Davis and a team of Arson Debris Specialist were still sifting through the rubble looking for evidence. 'He works with Stacey' Moses thought to himself "what the hell is going on" Moses said to himself 'this couldn't be a coincidence' he thought. Moses was concerned for the safety of Stacey, just then his cell-phone rang he picked it up off the seat and answered it "hello" he said "hi Moses I'm in trouble they want the flash-drive" it was Stacey and it sound like she was just crying "Stacey are you alright" he asked her "they said if you don't give them back the flash-drive they'll kill me" she said in a sobbing voice "don't worry I'm coming to get you" Moses told her as he backed out of the parking lot and on to the street. Stacey didn't reply "hello, hello" Moses said when he didn't hear anything on the other end of the line "Captain are you going to be the hero and save the day" it was General Banes "General if you hurt her I will kill you with a rock" Moses told him "well that's up to you Captain" General Banes said. "Tell me where you are and I'll be there" Moses asked him "you know where I am" the general replied "I'll be there in ten minutes" Moses told him "Captain if you made copies and sent them to any media outlet she's dead" General Banes warned him and then the line went dead. On the way to the coffee shop Moses actually stop into a stationery store where a friend of his worked and made a copy of the flash-drive but he wasn't going to tell the general that. His friend had a sister that worked at an office here for the President, Moses told his friend as soon as he can to send the copy to his sister and let her know to give it to President Myers, his friend agreed to it "I'll do that as soon as I can Mo" his friend said.

Moses was driving at a high rate of speed, running red-lights and swerving in and out of traffic 'the sooner I get there the better chance of keeping her alive' that's all he was thinking about (not Stacey, she didn't deserve this). Moses pulled into the main gate of the Space Lab, two security-guards stopped him at the gate to check his identification "can I see some I.D sir" one of the guards asked him. Moses took his wallet out of his pants pocket and showed them his license "thank you Mr.Uatobuu they're expecting you upstairs" the other guard told him. The steel front gate automatically opened up for Moses to drive in and so he did as he put his wallet back in his pocket.

They all gathered in the Cellular Transfer room up on the third level of the Space Lab, General Banes had Stacey tied to a chair with dock-tape around her mouth and two Janoesian soldiers holding AR-15 machine-guns in their hands standing over her. There was two steel-tables in the center of the room, one had a Ugandan Silverback gorilla strapped down on it. The large monkey was pasted out from the tranquilizer-darts the Janoesian soldiers shot into it. Through gene research Neilson knew that an unknown gene could function in a visiting host but it would have to be the opposite sex of the host if not there's a high chance that it may cause a pathogen. They all stood around Neilson as he explained minus General Banes the two soldiers and Stacey, "the primate on the table is a female Ugandan Silverback" he told them as he continued "in order for the cells to function it must be a male host" Neilson informed them as he prepped the gorilla for transfer.

Moses parked his truck in front of the Space Lab he grabbed the flash-drive from out of the glove-compartment and left. When Moses got in the front door lobby there was a guard sitting behind a desk to his immediate right, Moses went over to speak to the security-guard "hi my name is Moses" he said to the guard "yes Mr. Uatobuu, they're on the third floor in the Cellular Transfer room" the guard told him with a business-like smile on his face. Moses took one of the three elevators that were in the lobby up to the third floor, the elevator stopped at the third floor and Moses stepped out into the third floor lobby, it was a large open area with hallways to his right and left and two going off to his northeast and northwest direction. There was black signs on chains hanging from the ceiling in front the halls, Moses took the one that read Transfer Wing. Walking down the hallway Moses could see that it had different rooms to the left and right of it, he then came upon a room titled Cellular Transfer, Moses opened the door and went in the large room. Beyond the computer-screens and medical equipment in the distance he could see four figures standing around a table, Moses put the flash-drive in his pants pocket and moved in closer to see what was going on "hi I'm here to see General Banes" Moses said his unknown voice startled the group "hey how did you get past security, you can't be up here" Aaron told Moses as he turned around to see where the voice was coming from "tell him I have what he wants" Moses informed the group. "Welcome Captain, glad to see you made it safely" Moses heard a voice say to him from the other side of the room out of view, he turned around to see who it was, it was General Banes and he had Stacey tied up to a chair with two Janoesian soldiers holding guns to her head.

Moses took the flash-drive out of his pocket and raised it up in his hand so the general could see it "see General I'm holding up my end of the deal" Moses said to General Banes, the general smiled "good" he replied back to Moses, Stacey was mumbling something but because she had tape over her mouth Moses couldn't make out what she was saying. General Banes looked over at Neilson standing beside the table and then back at Moses "just hand it to Doctor Gainer over there" he told Moses as he motioned with his head where Doctor Gainer was standing, Moses looked at Stacey and then back at General Banes, he walked towards where Neilson was standing and handed him the flash-drive. As this exchange was happening through sweat and saliva Stacey managed to get the tape around her mouth to slip down below her chin "MO IT'S A TRAP" she shouted to Moses. Before Moses could turn around to hear what Stacey was saying Neilson gave him an injection in his neck causing him to pass out. When Moses woke up he was pinned down on the table next to the gorilla with steel bracelets around his wrist, ankles and neck, they were bolted to the table "what the hell is this" Moses asked General Banes who was now standing over top of him next to Neilson. "You are going to be our Guinea pig, look at it as you being apart of a great step forward in evolution" General Banes told him "don't do this general" Moses said as he helplessly tried to get out of his restraints "you won't getaway with this" he told the general. General Banes stood over top of Moses with his face close to his "I'm a four star general you'll be surprised on what I can getaway with" he told Moses "let Stacey go" Moses then told him "I'll let Doctor Gainer take over from here" General Banes said as he backed away from Moses "LET HER GO GENERAL" Moses shouted at him, the general went back over to where Stacey was. Neilson stood over Moses and placed a tray of syringes on the table "you need to calm down Mr. Uatobuu there's no way out of those restraints" he informed Moses "get the fuck away from me" Moses told him, the other scientist were watching at a close distance away as Neilson started the transformation process "they'll be four injections, two in the soft tissue and two in the bone-marrow the bone-marrow ones are going to hurt" he informed Moses. Neilson put a thick piece of gauze in Moses mouth so he doesn't bite his tonge "the transformation process should take up to ten minutes" Neilson told the other scientist. The four syringes on the tray were very large, Neilson picked one up and injected it in Moses shoulder and then he picked up another and injected it in his leg, Moses spit out the gauze "STOP!" he screamed at Neilson, one of the Janoesian soldiers intervened and picked up the gauze, put it back in Moses mouth and put dock-tape over his mouth "this should keep you quiet" the soldier told him as he backed away from the table. "these two injections were in the soft tissue" Neilson said as he continued with the transformation process, he picked up the last two syringes and stuck one in Moses neck and the other he stuck in Moses other leg, the last two syringes had longer and stronger needles on them they were meant to penetrate the bone and enter the marrow. A few minutes after he was injected the transformation effect started happening, Moses blood vessels started to pulsate, he screamed out in pain, his bones started contorting getting longer and bigger while this was happening his muscles were reacting the same way, additional muscle even started to grow on top of the muscles he already had. As Moses body structure got bigger his clothes tore off of him and strange gray and black hairs started growing all over his body, he started getting a severe headache as his skull and face expanded and got larger. At this time General Banes and his soldiers had taken Stacey to an above-ground delivery and loading zone around back where their van was parked, they had Stacey tied up in the back of the van with one of the soldiers guarding over her. After the transformation Moses had passed out on the table "the subject has now gone through the full transformation" Neilson said to the other scientist and continued "the time it took for the subject to fully transform is" Neilson looked at his watch "eleven minutes" he told the scientist. When Moses woke up Neilson was still talking to the group of scientist Moses couldn't move his body yet he just opened his eyes, he noticed that his arms weren't the same they were large and hairy like a gorilla, Moses looked down at his feet they looked like large hairy hands. Moses also noticed because his body frame grew so much it caused him to break free of his restraints. As soon as Moses body was free from paralysis he leaped up on the table he was just laying on, this action startled everyone into shear terror, Neilson turned around to see why everyone was scrambling for safety and as soon as he did so Moses swatted him aside with a heavy back handed slap that broke Neilson's jaw and shattered his ear-drum, it sent Neilson flying and crashing into a bunch of PC and Mainframe computers with such force that his limbs were twisted and broken causing him to resemble a beat-up rag-doll just laying there on the floor. Enraged Moses then broke a steel rod off a computer-stand and threw it like a javelin into the back of Aaron Fentcal just as he was about to exit the room, it went into his back and out his chest, about two feet of it pierced its way into a brick-wall. Moses was so angry all he could think about is if Stacey was okay, he started picking up computers and medical equipment and throwing them across the room, he stopped when he saw himself in a mirror that was on the wall beside him.

Moses turned and faced the mirror so he could get a better look at himself 'they turned me into a gorilla' he thought to himself, the only part of him that had some human features was his face and the fact that he was able to speak although his voice was now deep and amplified. Moses was bigger than the average gorilla he was eight feet five inches tall and weighed in at 600 pounds of solid muscle. Moses stood there looking at himself in the mirror as a bunch of electrical wires sparked a fire from all the chemicals that spilled on the floor, "motherfucker" Moses said to himself as he stood there staring at himself, the fire started getting bigger, Moses then turned around and picked up a Mainframe computer and threw it through the window like a soft-ball he then jumped through the window, just as he did that the whole Transfer Wing blow up. Moses landed in an oak-tree, he found himself holding on to the tree's branches with his feet he then started swinging with his hands and feet from tree to tree, he headed out in a small patch of forest towards the Turynfoymus Mountains. Moses couldn't believe how much at ease he was swinging from tree to tree and also at such a rate of speed (90 miles an hour) he screamed out in joy and excitement "WHOO WEE!" as he swung through the trees. He was now at the western region of the Black Forest close to the base of the Turynfoymus Mountains, Moses decided on taken a rest in a banyan-tree the only thing was is that the rest turned into a five hour snooze, when Moses woke up he realized that he was back to his human state and he was also naked. Moses jumped down out of the banyan-tree and went looking for a camping or picnicking area where he could steal a pair of pants, Moses kept off the beaten path so he wouldn't be seen by anyone, on his search Moses spotted through a cluster of short palm-trees a camp-ground, on the grounds a pair of pants was hanging on a clothes-line. Moses slowly made his way to the camp-ground, he hid behind a palm-tree waiting to see if anyone was around, there was a river nearby Moses could hear people laughing and talking by the river so he went and took the pants off the line and took off back into the cluster of palm-trees. With the pants rolled up under his arm Moses headed to a change-room he saw on his hunt for pants, when Moses got close to the change-room he came out of the bushes and walked down a foot-path, he didn't realize that there was two women hiking behind him. When the women saw his bare bottom bouncing as he walked down the path they started giggling to themselves, one of them snuck up behind him and slapped him on the ass this made Moses flinch in surprise, he turned around to see who it was, the lady smiled at him, Moses covered himself with his hands and ran to the change-room.

ADJUSTING TO TRANSFER

General Banes was at Tamerra Memorial Hospital under severe care in ICU, the surgeons had wired his jaw back together but he was still in a coma and he also had four broken ribs, whip-lash in his neck and a shattered knee-cap. He had barely made it out of the blast-radius of the explosion when the blast-waves hurled him up against a mahogany tree, the branches from the tree broke his jaw and ribs plus his head slammed into its trunk. One of the general's soldiers got decapitated in the explosion.

Stacey was on the second floor of Gordon Alan Central Hospital in north Tamerra, she was banged up pretty good, she was lucky she had no broken bones. All Stacey could remember about yesterday is that there was an explosion, Stacey was tied up in the back of a van when the explosion happened, the explosion caused the van to roll and end up against a brick-wall. Stacey was fine just unconscious at the time the soldier that was with her broke his neck as the van was rolling. The firemen used the jaws-of-life to get Stacey out of the van, now she had woken up in the hospital and all she could think about is if Moses was okay and where he was. One of Stacey's co-workers stood next to her bed, her name was Shelby Chamberlain she broadcasts the weather at TJNX news station, she was a good friend to Stacey "good afternoon" she said when Stacey opened her eyes, Stacey moaned as she rubbed her head with her hand "what time is it" she asked Shelby "almost 2pm" Shelby replied "how long have I been out" Stacey inquired "the doctors say almost eighteen hours" Shelby replied. Stacey looked up at Shelby "I would of expected to see Sedrick standing over me not you" Stacey said to her "didn't you hear Sedrick is dead, his house blew-up, they say it was a gas leek" Shelby informed Stacey "what! when did that happen" Stacey asked her shocked to hear the news "yesterday afternoon" Shelby replied "fuck" Stacey said to herself. "What's going on Stacey" Shelby asked her "what do you mean" Stacey said innocently "your co-workers at the news station want to know what's going on because there's soldiers right now at the news station looking for you" Shelby told Stacey. Stacey knew it was just a matter of time that they would come by the hospital and find her "you have to get me out of here Shelby" Stacey said with a concerned look on her face "why what's going on" Shelby asked her "I promise I'll tell you latter just please get me out of here" Stacey asked Shelby "how, the two policemen that came in with you are down the hall at the reception's desk right in front of the elevators" Shelby informed her. Stacey looked over her shoulder at the window next to her bed "how bout this window" Stacey said to Shelby "I don't know" Shelby replied sounding pretty wary "if not I'm going to end up dead" Stacey said to her "okay" Shelby said as she nodded her head. Stacey quickly gathered up her clothes off the chair that was on the other side of the bed, she gave them to Shelby to put in her bag.

A couple of high ranking officers and a group of the Janoesian Military Police came and took General Banes to the hospital on Base Laysan. The two high ranking officers signed his release-form, the general was wheeled out on a gurney still in a coma the military police had a van parked out in front of the hospital waiting to transport the general to Base Laysan.

Maureen Robertson and Remni Claus were rescued out of the rubble of the explosion by a group of firemen and taken by EMS to Tamerra Memorial Hospital to be checked out for any broken bones or concussions. On the day of the explosion Maureen and Remni had gotten in one of the elevators on the third floor and were taking it down to the ground floor when the explosion happened, this caused the elevator cables to snap and the elevator they were in came crashing down to the ground floor. It took a fireman with a blow-torch to get the elevator door open, when the door was opened they could see that Maureen and Remni weren't too banged up just a little shaken up. Maureen was sitting up in the hospital bed with her husband standing over her holding her hand. She was still shaken up by what she experienced yesterday, she started crying and her husband held her close "it's okay you're safe now" he assured her.

Gwen was at the beach listening to the radio on her laptop when the news of the explosion came over the radio. Yesterday when the explosion happened at the Space Lab she was already at home and later on she went to a nightclub with a friend of her's Ruth Onomauwae and was there for the whole night so she didn't hear anything about it until now, it was a surprise to her. Gwen was actually waiting for Ruth to show up, they were going to have lunch together at one of the bistros along the beach's boardwalk. Ruth lives in the same neighborhood as Gwen, she's a twenty-five year old native to the island that teaches at the local elementary school. Ruth is a very beautiful lady she stands at five feet seven inches tall with a slight hour-glass figure, she has a tawny-brown complexion with long mocha-brown hair that has large curls, her coffee-brown eyes seem to smile as she's looking at you. The news also said that the Janoesian Army was hunting something in the nearby woods around the Space Lab, Gwen wondered if she would be working on Monday because by what she sees on the news the army has the Space Lab on lock-down, only persons with government ID and clearance can enter 'what are they hiding' she thought to herself.

After Moses came out of the change room he was hiking along a beaten-path carpeted with wood-chips. He had been on the path for just over ten minutes, he felt relief in his bare feet walking on the moist wood-chips, this abled him to think clearer although his body still felt a little tired. Moses took his time walking on the path as his legs didn't feel up to par, he wondered what caused him to change back into his normal self 'was that the end of it or was there more to come' he thought to himself. On his journey along the beaten-path Moses stumbled upon a small stone silo with a black wooden door and two windows that were painted dark-green so no one could see what was inside, one of the windows were completely busted out. Moses looked at it as a place he could rest for awhile, he walked up to the door and saw a large pad-lock on it "shit" he said to himself disappointed that it was locked, he then noticed the broken window and smiled to himself. There was a tree stump under the window-sill, Moses stood on the stump and crawled in through the window. Inside the silo was dark, Moses found a light-switch and turned it on, the room lit up, right then he realized that it was a weapons-silo for the Janoesian Army, they had a stockpile of weapons in there, all sorts of weapons and ammunition. Moses looked around the silo in aw at all the weapons 'I might need some of these' he thought to himself, just in case he did turn into that beast again so he went around and took what he needed, he took a Bar Kukri sword along with the black-sheath it came with, a fifteen feet long brown braided leather whip with a silver trident tip and a Plain Round Carbon-Steel Battle Shield that had a razor sharp edge it came with a brown leather strap. Moses tossed the weapons that he took out the broken window he then crawled back out the window, he collected the weapons off the ground and left, he was going to hide them somewhere. Moses came upon an old-growth banyan tree he hid his newly found weapons inside the rooted trunk of the tree and covered them with dry leaves and peat moss, Moses felt drained like he didn't have any energy, he wondered if that was a symptom of his transformation. He sat for awhile with his back resting against the trunk of the banyan tree, he was thinking about Stacey.

Second in command to General Banes was Three Star General Robert Teal, General Teal was told by General Banes if anything went wrong during the transformation process of the Primate Program that he should call Doctor Ray Gatlain an animal surgeon that works at The Farm in Bayamo, Cuba and he would get in touch with a Jessepi Montoya a large game hunter, and that's exactly what General Teal did.

The Farm is a wildlife preserve that covers twenty acres of land it is located in Bayamo, Cuba and its soul purpose is to capture animals and sell their organs or whatever is valuable on the black-market. There are thirty poachers that work at The Farm most of them are large game hunters, Jessepi Montoya is considered to be one of the best out of all of them. Jessepi Montoya is from Bayamo, he's thirty-seven years old, he speaks English and Spanish and was educated in the United States, he stand at six feet tall and weighs 200 pounds most times when you see him he's wearing a Tigris Draconis Multicam Poncho over a khaki-brown short sleeve shirt a brown leather outback hat with chin cord on his head, black knee length cargo shorts and brown Timberland hiking boots.

Ray Gatlain was sitting behind his desk in his office at The Farm, he was on the phone with General Teal "hi Robert I was hoping to hear from General Banes" he said to General Teal, "oh I see that's too bad, I hope he gets better" he said after hearing General Teal's reply. "Okay I'll give Jessepi a call right now" Ray told General Teal, Ray hung up the phone and called Jessepi, Jessepi was in the Congo Basin hunting the African forest elephants, after catching a few of them they would be transported back to The Farm to have their tusk removed so they could be sold on the black-market. After taking their tusk he would give the rest of the animal to Ray so he could remove any valuable organs. Whatever meat was leftover from the animal was sold to grocery-stores all over the world including independent meat shops. Jessepi and his gang of hunters set up base-camp along the Ubangi Rivers, the camp was quarantined off, there was a thirty feet hi steel barbed-wire fence surrounding the whole camp that was plug into seventy-five thousand volts of electricity. Jessepi was behind a desk loading his SAR 80 assault rifle when the phone rang 'I wonder who that is' he thought to himself as he answered his cell-phone "yeah yeah" he said to the caller "we're in secondary protocol" Ray said to him, Jessepi recognized Ray Gatlain's voice

"I understand sir" Jessepi replied and ended the call. Jessepi called over one of the hunters he came to Africa with, he motioned with his hand for him to come over. It was Kelso Ramirez a hunter of buffalo, bison and rhinoceros, he uses a compound bow made of ox-horn and hickory that shoots arrows made of steel and iron-wood. Kelso was helping some men get a large net under an elephant so they could transport the animal when he heard Jessepi whistling for him, he told the men that he had to go and went over to see what Jessepi wanted.

After breaking Stacey out of the hospital Shelby drove her to her place in the northern section of AquaHorn Beach. Shelby lived in a two bedroom bungalow that back patio overlooked the Atlantic ocean, she inherited the house after her parents pasted away. The neighborhood Shelby lived in was a culdesac of five houses that back patios overlooked a bluff, Shelby backed her car onto her driveway and put it in park. She helped Stacey out of the car and assisted her to the front door, Shelby opened the door to her house and closed it behind her as she continued to assist Stacey to a couch in the living room "thank you" Stacey said to her as she laid on her back in the couch. "Would you like something to drink" Shelby asked Stacey "just a glass of water please" Stacey replied, Shelby was still concerned about what was going on and Stacey's health, she turned around and headed into the kitchen. Stacey laid there on the couch with her head proped up on it's arm, she looked at the ceiling thinking about Moses and feeling guilty for getting him involved in this thing "I hope you're alright Mo" she said to herself. Shelby came back to the living room with a glass of water in her hand, Stacey sat up in the couch as Shelby served her the glass of water, "what now" Shelby asked in a coy way "well I'm going to need a place to stay for a few days" Stacey said to Shelby "okay" Shelby replied "and a hot bath" Stacey continued "you know you're always welcomed here" Shelby replied. Stacey finished off her water and put the empty glass on a small night-table that was next to the couch "now will you tell me what's going on" Shelby asked her "I will tell you I just need some rest now" she said to Shelby "okay I'll grab you some blankets" Shelby told her.

Kelso came up to Jessepi and they shook hands and patted each other on the shoulders "how's everything going here, are you doing well" Jessepi asked Kelso "I can't complain this is what I do" Kelso replied as he smiled and patted himself on the chest "that's good because we got more work coming our way" Jessepi informed him "I'm with you all the way partner" Kelso said with assurance as he places his hand on Jessepi's shoulder. "By the way what are we hunting" Kelso asked Jessepi "I don't know" Jessepi replied, Kelso stood there looking at him trying to quickly read Jessepi's thoughts, he finally said something "okay do we know the location" he asked Jessepi "it's on Janoesha Harbour" Jessepi replied "this should be good we're going to somewhere we've never been before to hunt an unknown creature" Kelso commented sarcastically "this hunt is different" Jessepi told him, Kelso knew right away what Jessepi meant by that. "The general wants us in Janoesha Harbour by tomorrow afternoon" Jessepi told Kelso and continued "so gather up the team we have a helicopter to catch" Jessepi informed him.

After sitting and thinking things over for a while Moses went hiking through the Black Forest, when he had gotten back to the banyan-tree he had collected a few items of clothing plus he had a plastic-bag filled with freshly picked fruits. Moses put down the bag of fruit on a patch of grass that grew next to the banyan-tree he then sat down with his back up against the banyan-tree and put the stack of clothes down beside him. On top of the stack was a pair of hiking-boots, on his journey through the Black Forest Moses had found them at an abandon campsite, they were his size so he took them. Moses held the boots in his hand while he examined them 'not in bad condition' he thought to himself, he tried them on and they fit like a glove so he laced them up and got to his feet and walked around to see how they felt "comfortable, very comfortable" he smiled to himself. Moses then grabbed from the stack of clothes a blue-rayon button-up shirt and put it on. He was planning on heading to Sharesta Plains the closest town he could get supplies. Sharesta Plains is a small town located a couple miles south of Sharesta Gardens, Moses took two passion-fruit out of the plastic-bag and put them on the stack of clothes he then grabbed his sword and whip just in case, before he left he grabbed the passion-fruits off the stack of clothes. It was going to be a long hike but Moses could handle it now that he's well rested plus he trained out here back when he was in the army, speaking of the army he imagines that they would be looking for him right about now, doing there policy grid-searches and getting nowhere. Moses knew every inch of the Black Forest and also knew places to hide.

General Teal had deployed a jungle-unit of the Janoesian Army on the Black Forest their instructions were to go in and flush out, capture or eliminate the problem. General Teal was also waiting for Jessepi Montoya, he sent a couple of his soldiers to pick Jessepi up from James Starr when his plane lands, he had set Jessepi up with accommodations in the small town of Beryl Rado a suburb of Pearles that sits south of the Black Forest. Beryl Rado is known for it's marsh land also the Sambar Horn River goes through it, the town has problems with caiman, there has been six caiman attacks so far this year, four of them involved children. He heard from Ray that Jessepi is a professional and one of the best in the world, he's well known for capturing three lions in southern Sudan, one male lion and two female. General Teal was sitting at the bar of a local pub that was located on Base Laysan, he was drinking a mix of freshly squeezed pine-apple juice with two shots of Wray & Nephew 150 proof rum. He was thinking about General Banes, him and Terrance knew each other for years all the way back to when they were in Young Rangers together. Robert heard from a doctor at the hospital that Terrance was still in a coma, this didn't sit well with Robert 'not only that the army may lose a great general but I might lose a friend' he thought to himself. Robert finished off whatever he had left in his rock-glass and asked the bartender for another "sure thing" the bartender replied. Robert was determined to capture or kill the person responsible for this monstrosity, the bartender came back with a full rock-glass he placed it on a coaster in front of Robert "thanks" Robert said "not a problem" the bartender replied.

The Gregory Act

The Gregory Act was written into Janoesian law on August 30th 1970, the Act was named after Claude Gregory a police officer that was

killed in the line of duty by a gang member.
The Act states that anyone male or female that
has a college diploma or a university degree
and is looking for a job in their field of study
or a job in general cannot be affiliated or a
member of a street gang or organized gang,
if they are they will not be hired. The Act
also prohibits anyone male or female that is
affiliated or a member of a street or organized
gang from becoming a politician regardless
if the person has a clean criminal record.

Stacey woke up from her nap on the couch, she stretched and yawned out of her slumber she remembered that she was not at the hospital she was at Shelby's place. Stacey sat up in the couch and wiped the sleep out of her eyes and then looked around the living room for Shelby. Shelby was in the kitchen preparing something to eat she felt hungry after reading a chapter of a Danielle Steele novel, she was still very concerned about what Stacey got herself into. She heard the TV turn on in the living room so she knew that Stacey had woken up, Shelby finished making her cold-cut sandwiches and went to the living room to eat them. Stacey was watching the news, on the news Janet Jacobson was speaking with Audrey Boyner the late Neilson Gainer's assistant, they were just outside the front gate of the Space

Lab. Audrey wasn't in the Space Lab at the time of the explosion, on the news Stacey could see that she had been crying "we're here with Audrey Boyner an employee at the Space Lab, Miss Boyner can you tell us what went on here" Janet asked her "well I'm not too sure I wasn't in the building at the time, all I was told by Doctor Gainer is that they were working on a different strain of DNA" Audrey replied "Are you referring to Neilson Gainer" Janet inquired "yes" Audrey replied "witnesses say they saw a large ape-like creature leave the Space Lab and ran off into the woods behind the Lab do you know anything about this" Janet asked Audrey "no" Audrey replied not knowing what Janet was talking about. Stacey stared at the TV in shock "oh my God" she said to herself "what have they done to you Moses", Shelby came in the living room with a plate full of turkey-sandwiches, she sat down in the couch next to Stacey and put the plate on the small center piece table in front of them "I made some sandwiches if you're hungry" she told Stacey "thank you" Stacey said to her. "So how are you feeling" Shelby asked Stacey "I feel a little better, that nap actually helped" Stacey replied, Shelby looked over at the TV and saw that Stacey was watching the news "anything good on the news" Shelby asked Stacey looking to lead into a question. Stacey looked at Shelby trying to read her face for any trace of sarcasm, Shelby gave her a innocent smile "no just the same old thing" Stacey replied "is there anything you want to talk about" Shelby inquired "not that I know of" Stacey replied as she picked up a sandwich trying to prevent eye-contact "what's going on" Shelby asked her sharply "okay I'll tell you" Stacey said to her "me and Sedrick broke into the Space Lab because I got a scoop on corruption that was happening at the Space Lab and in my investigation I took a flash-drive from the Space Lab that has some sensitive files on it, that is why the army is looking for me and I believe that is why Sedrick is dead" Stacey looked at Shelby to see what she thought of it all "how can I help" Shelby asked with a look of concern "first I need you to help me find my boyfriend Moses Uatobuu, I think they've done something to him" Stacey said "sure" Shelby replied.

Moses had been hiking for near over an hour, he was now on an old logging road he saw a green wooden sign in the distance marked Sharesta Plains so he kept walking in the same direction. As he was walking he was thinking about Stacey, he couldn't live with himself if anything happened to her, he hoped she wasn't there when the explosion happened at the Space Lab. Although he didn't want to think that way Moses was hoping that General Banes had left the Space Lab with Stacey before the explosion happened. Moses could now see the town of Sharesta

Plains just beyond a cluster of palm-trees and bushes, the main road that went through Sharesta Plains was dirt mixed with gravel. As Moses walked into the town he could see parked out in front of a bookstore a jeep from the Janoesian Army, no one was in the jeep. Moses went into a barber-shop and watched and waited to see if any soldiers would come out of the bookstore, he stood there inside the barber-shop peeking through its large display-window from behind a red curtain. From behind the curtain he could see a soldier step out of the variety store that was just three stores down from the bookstore, the soldier was holding in his hand an AR-15 light machine-gun, he was walking up towards the jeep. When the soldier got to the jeep he sat in the front passenger seat, Moses knew where there is one there's more to come so he stood behind the curtain waiting to see if there were more soldiers "can I help you sir" one of the two barbers in the shop asked him "thanks I'm okay I'm just waiting for my girlfriend" Moses replied. Moses thought that the army might be doing a sweep, searching every small town in and around the Black Forest region. Moses sat down in one of the chairs in the barber-shop that was in front of the curtain trying to look inconspicuous, he turned his body in the chair to get a better look at what was going on outside. Moses saw two soldiers exit out of the bookstore and head towards the jeep, when they got to the jeep one sat in the driver's seat and one sat in the backseat. Moses then got up out of his seat and went over to talk to one of the barbers "is there a back door in here" he asked the short hefty barber "it's just down the hall there past the washrooms" the barber pointed. Moses headed down the hall and out the door that had an exit sign over top of it, he then ran into another soldier patrolling the area, before the soldier could react Moses immediately grabbed the soldier's rifle and spun him around using the soldier's own body weight and giving him a elbow to the jaw that knocked him out. Moses threw the soldier's rifle in some nearby bushes and took his CB-radio, he then started to walk down the back alley of the line of stores in the opposite direction that the jeep was facing. When he got to the end of the plaza he went around front to see where the jeep was, Moses could see that it was parked at the same spot, it never moved, then a voice came over the CB-radio that Moses had "corporal report, Nickols come in" it was saying. Moses knew that they would be going to check on their man, so he decided on heading back into the woods for now and waiting it out. When he got to the woods just outside the town he climbed up a Ficus citrifolia tree and waited for the army to do their sweep of the town. As he was sitting in the tree watching and waiting to see when the coast was clear two soldiers holding machine-guns came to the tree, they stood there underneath him smoking a cigarette unaware that he was in the tree. Moses couldn't have them just standing there smoking because sooner or later they would look up and discover him in the tree so he jumped out of the tree and tackled both of them to the ground, while they were on the ground he kicked one in the head knocking him out and the other one he cut off one of his arms with his sword. Moses was about to take off running when he saw a group of soldiers come out from the bushes around him, they circled around him aiming their machine-guns at him "freeze don't move" one of them ordered him "lay on the ground" another one told him. Moses looked around trying to figure away out, that's when one of them tried to throw a net over him, Moses stomach started to hurt and his head began aching, his body started to contort and grow as his muscles got bigger. His transformation only took under two minutes to complete, he had changed back into the creature, just then he did a ground-roll, jumped up and swatted a soldier across the face decapitating him all in one motion. He then jumped in a nearby tree as the other soldiers unloaded gun-fire on him, he swung from tree to tree trying his best to getaway from them but two army jeeps were following under him unloading gun-fire as he swung through the trees. The soldiers chased Moses to an open area near the banks of the Sambar Horn River, there was no more trees for Moses to hide in so he jumped out of the banyan tree he was in and landed in one of the jeeps, before the four soldiers that occupied the jeep could recover from the initial impact that Moses caused he cut them to ribbons with his sword. When the soldiers in the other jeep seen the slaughter of their fellow comrades they unloaded gun-fire on Moses which didn't seem to have any effect on him, Moses saw that their bullets weren't effecting him, he took the whip from around his neck and whipped it out and with a loud snap it disarmed the machine-guns out of the hands of two soldiers the other two stopped shoot and stood there in the jeep staring in aw at Moses as he leaped over to the other side of the river and into another trees where he began swinging from tree to tree again.

The Janoesian army sent a Boeing CH-47 Chinook helicopter to pick-up Jessepi and his men from the Congo Basin and fly them into Janoesha Harbour. It would take them a half an hour to fly over from the Congo, their pick-up point on Janoesha Harbour is a landing strip just outside James Starr Airport. Along with Jessepi came Kelso Ramirez and Bruno Ellk, Bruno Ellk is a thirty-five year old ex-Spanish soldier from Malaga, Spain that got stranded in the Ugandan mountains just around the base of Stanley Mountain after the carrier-jet crashed carrying him and his crew, the two pilots died on impact but Bruno and his unit survived, they were stranded for nine months no one knew where they were the radio in the cockpit of the jet got destroyed after the jet cot on fire and blew-up. That is where Bruno learned to hunt and kill sufficiently, he really specialized in killing and capturing African buffalo and East African lions, he got so good at it that Jessepi saw him on one of his captures and after hired him onto his crew. Jessepi wasn't to sure what he was up against 'if I find out that I need more men I can always get them' he thought to himself. Prior to the flight Jessepi was informed that there would be someone at the landing strip to pick-up him and his men and drive them to Beryl Rado "how long until we land" Kelso asked Jessepi, well aware that Jessepi had all the answers "a little under a half an hour" Jessepi replied. "So is this your first real adventure out of Africa" Kelso turned and ask Bruno trying to get a feel for him, checking to see if he's the real deal "was on the Gaza Strip for awhile" Bruno chuckled, laughing off Kelso's attempt to buff up next to him, Kelso smiled to himself and continued to play with his handmade Damascus hunting knife on the seat next to him. After just under a half an hour of flying over the Atlantic the helicopter landed on an air-strip built for weather-planes and single-engine Cessnas located just east of James Starr Airport. The helicopter came to a safe landing and opened up its doors the three men came walking down the steps of the helicopter to the ground level with Jessepi leading the way. A black 1951 Lincoln Cosmopolitan limousine was waiting there to pick them up and drive them to Beryl Rado "nice car" Kelso said as he stared at the limo, the men put their luggage in the trunk of the limo, there chauffeur for the journey also helped, it would take them forty-five minutes to drive to Beryl Rado, the men all got in the car and it sped off. As the limo got further and further away from the landing-strip it entered onto Route 23 into Pearles, Jessepi had never been to Janoesha Harbour before he just heard about it from Doctor Gatlain when he was at the Farm. Bruno was going through the limo's liquor-fridge "no drinking on this job we need to keep a clear head" Jessepi told him, Bruno put back the bottle of gin he took out of the fridge "sorry" he said.

The evening came down on Tamerra and the sun was slowly hiding its self behind the Turynfoymus mountains, Stacey and Shelby was sitting out on Shelby's front porch in a couple of fold-out lawn-chairs. They had packed two backpacks with rope, flashlights, small plastic-bags, two camcorders and a hand-gun, Shelby was reluctant to bring the gun but Stacey grabbed it anyway. "Okay I think the first place to look will be the Space Lab" Stacey told Shelby "I think that's a bad idea Stacey" Shelby replied "why is that" Stacey asked her "because they have that place under heavy security and those soldiers are looking for you" Shelby answered "yeah I know but that's the last place he was and we have to pick up his trail from there" Stacey told her. It did make sense to Shelby but she was concerned about Stacey's safety, she nodded and smiled at Stacey "okay" she said to her, so they went and got into Shelby's car. Shelby started up the car and backed it out of her driveway, she drove along Route 55 and then exited left onto Route 22, she stayed on Route 22. "So where are you planning on looking when we get there" Shelby asked Stacey "we were in one of the back offices which windows face the back of the building so we'll start there" Stacey replied "back of the building" Shelby asked confusingly looking for clarity "yes" Stacey answered. They were getting close to where Stacey's condo is, as they got closer Stacey could see a couple of Janoesian soldiers standing out in the front lobby "slow down a bit" she told Shelby, Shelby complied "doesn't look like you can go home either" Shelby said sarcastically, Stacey gave her a serious look "sorry" Shelby apologized. Stacey watched and saw as an additional group of soldiers came out of the building and got into a black SUV, the two soldiers standing at the lobby stayed there. "Come on lets go there's nothing more to see here" Stacey told Shelby so they drove off and continued on route to the Space Lab.

Moses continued to swing through the trees until he was far away from those soldiers, he stopped at a clearing in the forest where a pond was to get a drink. He sat on a large rock that was protruding out of the pond he started scooping up water in his hand and drinking it. He hadn't changed back to his normal self, his heart was beating at a thousand miles per hour, Moses sat there drinking water and trying to calm himself down just then he saw a bunch of birds fly out of a Geiger tree, he sensed something was coming and not long after he saw a tank from the Janoesian army ride over bushes and through some tall grass and stop at the other side of the pond, a voice spoke through a loud-speaker "GIVE YOURSELF UP THERE'S NOWHERE TO GO WE HAVE THE PLACE SURROUNDED" the voice ordered Moses. Moses stood up on the rock and started beat his chest continuously with his fist signifying that he was ready for anything, he then saw soldiers coming out from behind trees, they were holding machine-guns, Moses let out a loud roar and began running on his hands and legs around the pond towards the soldiers. The soldiers unloaded gunfire on him but Moses dodged the bullets and when he got close enough to them he took his sword out of its sheath that was strapped behind his back and decapitated some of the soldiers, the tank tried its best to shoot him but Moses leaped up on top of it and bent back its gun so it could only fire at its self. The other soldiers ran for cover as they kept firing at Moses, Moses threw his sword into one of the soldiers back, the force of the throw propelled the soldier forward and stuck in a palm-tree with the soldier pinned up against the tree slowly dying.

On their way to the Space Lab Shelby turned on the radio to listen to some music, the first station it was on was the news, Shelby was about to change the station when Stacey touched her hand and told her not to "I want to hear this" Stacey said to her so Shelby turned up the volume a bit. The radio was saying that the Janoesian Army was searching for something in the western and central Black Forest regions they didn't say what the army was looking for but Stacey had a good idea who it was, the radio warned that if there are people camping, fishing or hiking in the Black Forest to vacate the area as quickly as possible and if they see anything suspicious to report it to a ranger or a soldier that's close by. "What's that all about" Shelby asked Stacey "I think we should probably head out to the Black Forest" Stacey replied "I don't think that's a good idea" Shelby said "that's Moses out there and their out to kill him or capture him" Stacey explained to her. Shelby was very reluctant to drive out to the Black Forest "with all those soldiers there, there's a very good chance that you could be arrested" she told Stacey "yeah but I need to know that Moses is okay" Stacey told her "you truly love him" Shelby then said "yes I do" Stacey replied. Shelby smiled to herself indulging in the reality of true love "in that case we'll head out to the Black Forest" she told Stacey as she made a detour on Route 50 going northbound. It would take them about thirty minutes to drive out there, on their drive out there Stacey didn't say much she rolled down her window and stared outside at the natural beauty of the countryside as fresh air blew through her hair. She was thinking about Moses hoping that he was not hurt, she wanted to get to him before they got to him, she had a pretty good idea what they wanted him for and she was going to do everything in her power to not let that happen "don't worry it's going to be okay" Shelby assured her as she glanced over at Stacey looking out the passenger side window, Stacey didn't reply.

The limo drove up the dirt driveway of a stone cabin and stopped in front of its wooden porch, Jessepi and his men got out of the car the chauffeur opened the trunk by pressing a button on the dashboard and then exited the car to help the men with their gear. They walked up the porch's steps to the front door of the cabin, they put all their gear on the porch as the chauffeur took a set keys out of his pants pocket and opened the front door for them, the chauffeur handed Jessepi the keys and told him that one of the keys was for the 2017 Jeep Wrangler parked in the back of the cabin. "Is there anything else I can help you with sir" the chauffeur asked Jessepi "no we're good" Jessepi replied, the chauffeur left them and got back into the limo and drove away. The men started carrying their gear into the cabin, Jessepi radioed in to let General Teal know that they arrived safely, after all their gear was inside the men sat in the living room on the couch, inside the cabin was fully furnished. "It's nice in here" Kelso said sitting in the couch as he put his feet up on a center piece table in front of him "get some rest men tomorrow bright and early we have to meet up with General Teal in the central Black Forest region" Jessepi informed them. Bruno was in the kitchen fishing through the fridge for something to eat he took out a loaf of bread, a tub of butter and a slab of roast-beef that was on a small platter and placed them on the counter next to him. He started making a sandwich, he was hungry from the flight and drive here, he made two sandwiches and put them on a small plate he then went back to the fridge now looking for something to drink and found a six pack of Sprite on the bottom shelf of the fridge, he took one and sat around the counter on a stool and ate his sandwiches.

After Moses retrieved his sword he headed back to the banyan-tree where he stashed the rest of his weapons, his plan to get supplies from Sharesta Plains had to wait there was too much soldiers around there. It was nighttime now and Moses was thinking about getting some rest he still knew that the army would be patrolling throughout the night so when he got back to where he stashed his weapons he took all his weapons and stored them up in the banyan tree. He then gathered up dry twigs and sprinkled them in the area around the banyan tree, this would allow him to hear who was coming while he was resting. Moses then climbed up into the banyan tree and sat on a large branch with his back resting up against the tree's trunk and there's where he slept for the rest of the night, while Moses was sleeping he changed back to his normal self.

As the sun rouse up over the Turynfoymus Mountains and shined down on the Black Forest General Teal and a platoon of soldiers commanded by a Lieutenant David Janes were waiting for Jessepi and his men to arrive. General Teal made sure the platoon had enough fire-power to take down Moses, he wasn't going to leave the Black Forest without killing or capturing Moses. General Teal stood beside a tank and lit a cigar, he took a couple puffs and blew the smoke out "fine day for a battle" he said to himself as he looked up into the sky "sir my men are in position and ready" Lieutenant Janes informed him "thank you lieutenant tell them to stand down for now" General Teal told him. "Sir I also brought a map of the central

Black Forest region" the lieutenant added, Lieutenant Janes had a canopy setup, under the canopy was a fold-out table on the table was the map, the men stood around the table looking at the map "the only way he could escape is along the banks of the Sambar Horn River" Lieutenant Janes informed General Teal "then lets get some men stationed along there" the general told him. "We have men going there right now sir" Lieutenant Janes said "excellent, lieutenant I want everyone on point if you have to kill him do so but try your best to bring him back alive" General Teal told him "yes sir" Lieutenant Janes replied as he saluted the general and left the canopy. General Teal stood there smoking his cigar and studying the map for any holes he was looking to see if he overlooked anything, just then Jessepi and his men pulled up in a Jeep Wrangler, Jessepi was driving he parked the jeep beside a Sabal palm-tree and hopped out of the driver's seat "wait here" he told his men. Jessepi walked over to where General Teal was "good morning general" Jessepi said as he entered under the canopy, General Teal looked up from staring at the map "good to see you made it" General Teal said to Jessepi. Jessepi put both his hands on the table as he stood over the map "so where are we at on this" he asked the general referring to the capture of Moses "well if you're referring to the capture of Silverback he will be boxed in if he enters the central Black

Forest area" General Teal replied as he took a couple puffs of his cigar and blew out the smoke. Jessepi was confused at the name General Teal mentioned "Silverback" Jessepi asked, the general nodded yes as he continued to smoke his cigar "what exactly are we hunting here" Jessepi inquired "from what I understand it's part human and part Silver-back gorilla so are you up for the challenge" General Teal replied "I have no problem with that" Jessepi told him "good, I thought you brought more men" the general asked him "they're waiting in the jeep" Jessepi replied. Jessepi looked at the map and studied it with the general "so what do you want us to do" Jessepi asked the general "find where it is and flush it out so it heads this way" General Teal replied.

It was Monday and still no word from the Space Lab letting her know if she's working today so Gwen decided to meet up with Ruth and go watch a Big Ticket Movie at the theater. Throughout the spring and summer seasons there are theaters on the island that show newly release movies for six dollars this includes a small popcorn and drink, the theaters are named BTM Cinemas most of them are along the beaches, they were built to attract tourist, some of them have rooftop patios with bar and serve finger-food. Gwen planned on going by Ruth's place and then they would go to the theater, she walked over to where Ruth's house was, Ruth lived in a quaint little bungalow at the end of a dead-end road the property around the house was so open and spacious it was perfect for someone with a dog. Ruth bought the house and rents a room out to a gentleman that works as a commercial electrician, the extra money helps her pay the mortgage each months. Ruth left the door to the back patio open, she was in the backyard sitting in a lawn-chair reading a Martha Grimes novel, this was one of Ruth's recreational past-times is to cuddle up to a good novel while she drank a cup of coffee and indulged in the outdoor serenity of her backyard. While she read Ruth liked to listen to a group of Red-legged Thrush chirping in a Wodyetia palm-tree, this is how she escaped from the chaos of the big city. Ruth heard the chime of her door-bell, she marked the spot in her book and got up from where she was sitting, she placed the book on the lawn-chair and headed for the front door. When she got to the front door she looked through the small window on the door, it was Gwen, Ruth opened the door "hi" she said to Gwen with a smile, Gwen replied with a smile of her own and then they hugged each other. Ruth invited Gwen in and they went out to the backyard "so still nothing from your workplace" Ruth asked Gwen as she offered her a lawn-chair to sit in "no nothing yet" Gwen replied as she sat down "the news said that they won't let anyone in without government clearance" Ruth said "yeah I heard that to, I just wonder how long this is going to be for" Gwen said to Ruth "I can't see it going on very much longer" Ruth said trying to keep Gwen thinking positive. Gwen brought a newspaper with her she was going to look through it's entertainment section for any newly released movie playing at the BTM Theater. She put the paper on her lap and flipped through it's pages looking for the entertainment section which didn't take her too long to find. Gwen and Ruth were into action adventure movies that have a happy ending "hopefully they have something good playing this time of day" Gwen said "BTM is always a good choice, if there's no movie to watch we can always hangout at their restaurant" Ruth assured her. "What about Fast and Furious 9" Gwen asked Ruth, Ruth made a funny face "hmm, is there anything else" she replied "how about Black Widow" Gwen inquired "that sounds good" Ruth told her "okay Black Widow it is" Gwen agreed "I guess for six dollars you can't go wrong" Ruth chuckled.

Stacey and Shelby slept overnight in Shelby's car that was parked in front of a diner/motel, Stacey had reclined her seat back to get a goods night rest and Shelby had her head resting on the driver's side door. Shelby opened her eyes slowly as the sun shined through the car's windshield, she yawned and tried to stretch the sleep out of her body but there wasn't enough room so she opened the door and got out of the car. She stood beside the car stretching her arms and legs so her body would wake up from its feeling of slumber, after a session of stretching her limbs she went back in the car and started looking for any new messages on her cell-phone. While Shelby was on her cell-phone Stacey was moaning in her seat as if she were dreaming suddenly her eyes opened and she sat up in her seat she turned and looked beside her and saw Shelby sitting there on her phone "good morning" Shelby said as she looked up from her phone at Stacey. As Stacey wiped the sleep from her eyes she realized what was happening (they had parked here overnight on their way to the central Black Forest region) "where are we" she asked Shelby "we're about fifteen minutes north of the town of Beryl Rado" Shelby replied "we should probably get something to eat and then get back on the road" Stacey told Shelby "don't you remember last night" Shelby asked Stacey "no, why" Stacey replied "because we went into that motel last night to asked about a room and the manager told us that the Janoesian Army reserved all the rooms for their soldiers, a truck load of them should be by at 10:00am" Shelby informed her. Stacey looked at her watch "that gives us only twenty-five minutes to get out of here" Stacey said to Shelby, Shelby shut the driver's side door and started up the car, Stacey put her seat back to its normal position, Shelby turned back onto the main road which was

Route 23. They had done their best to stay clear of the Janoesian Army so far but Stacey didn't know how long their luck would keep up, after all they were entering the Black Forest and it would be wise to anticipated a large military presence "we need to hide this car as soon as we get to the Black Forest" she told Shelby "okay and then what" Shelby asked Stacey confused about her demand "from there we hike on foot" Stacey replied. As they were driving along Route 23 Stacey saw a large army-truck filled with soldiers going in the opposite direction "they must be headed to that motel" Shelby said as she spotted them in her rear-view mirror, up ahead she saw the sign for Highway 31 north so she made a left turn onto it, this road would take them right into the Black Forest. Stacey knew that they couldn't get too close to the front entrance of the Black Forest that there would definitely be soldiers there so they planned to hide the car off the road under some fallen branches and leaves from a palm-tree, and that's exactly what they did. Stacey and Shelby collected what they needed from the car and started hiking "it's a good thing I didn't wear my heels today" Shelby said jokingly trying to lighten up the mood and not doing a good job at it, Stacey gave her a blank stare "sorry not the best place for humor" Shelby apologized. They both carried a backpack each as they hiked through the Black Forest, Stacey was holding a detailed map of the Black Forest rolled up in her hand "I take it you know where you're going" Shelby asked Stacey as she walked behind her "yeah somewhat" Stacey replied. Where they were was filled with marsh-land and tall grass the density of trees made it hard to see the open sky as the shadow from their leaves dappled the ground below, Stacey and Shelby found a beaten path to walk on, it was carpeted with wood-chips and mulch. "Be careful" Stacey told Shelby "okay, why" Shelby asked her with concern "because there's a lot of wild animals around here" Stacey replied "thank you for the heads up" Shelby said as she looked around tactfully.

Moses woke up and nearly fell out of the banyan-tree but before that happened he realized where he was and quickly regained his balance, Moses sat up in the banyan-tree with his back still braced up against its trunk. His body was still sore and tired from the night before, he stood up on the branch he was sitting on looking to make his way out of the tree but first he looked down at the area below him inspecting it for any disturbance (it looked the same as he left it). Moses climbed down out of the tree, he planned to change his location 'last night was too close for comfort' he thought to himself. He went into the tree's large series of roots to collect his weapons, he grabbed his sword and sheath and wore them behind his back and then rolled up his whip and hung on to it, he took his shield and wore it around his left forearm. Moses left his old hiding area and was looking for a new place to nest, the pare of pants that he stole was no longer a pare of pants they were now shorts, they had torn apart during his transformation. He stayed off the beaten path doing his best to keep out of the eye-site of the Janoesian Army, Moses came upon a small creek where he knelt down to get a drink of water. He knelt there washing the sleep out of his eyes planning what he was going to do today, in the middle of his thoughts he heard the motor of a vehicle nearby he then backed away from the creek and hid behind a palm-bush out of its view, the vehicle stopped and parked in front of the creek about seventy feet down from where Moses was. Moses peaked out from behind the bushes and saw that it was only an RV he then thought to himself 'maybe they had food' Moses was hungry he hadn't eating for awhile and this was his chance for a bite to eat. He didn't know how many people were in the RV but it wouldn't hurt to give whatever he was going to do a shot, what Moses was planning on doing was to steal some food out of the RV his only concern was how many people was in there, he didn't want to create any attention to himself 'this would have to be a covert operation' he thought to himself. Moses saw a young couple with a small boy come out of the RV the boy was holding a fishing-rod and so was the young man, the lady was holding a lawn-chair in which she folded out and sat on next to the creek while the young man and boy sat on a large rock baiting their hooks. Moses could see that they were far enough away from the RV to bring this plan into action, he stooped down next to bushes and behind trees quickly making his way to the back of the RV he stayed there watching and waiting for the right time when he could make a run for its door. Moses saw his opportunity when the young lady went and hugged the little boy, congratulating him for baiting his hook properly, Moses quickly made his way into the RV the RV looked bigger inside than outside. Moses opened up the small bar-like fridge that was in the RV he saw two Philly-steak sandwiches wrapped in plastic on the top shelf of the fridge, he took them and also grabbed two bottles of Blue Toucan and shut the fridge. He went back to the door of the RV and peeked out it's small window to see if the coast was clear, it was, the family was busy fishing in the creek so Moses made his exit and then ran off into the bushes. As Moses hiked around looking for a new location to hide his weapons he unwrapped one of the steaks and started eating it, he was so hungry and losing energy, this sandwich would put back some energy in his body. It didn't take him long to eat the Philly-steak, after eating one he put the other in his pocket for later and opened up a bottle of Blue

Toucan, because he didn't have any water on him he nursed the bottle of beer and put the other one in his back pocket. Moses had been hiking for a good fifteen minutes he was getting closer to the central Black Forest region just then he heard the sound of a helicopter above, he looked up to see what it was, it was a army helicopter 'it's flying pretty low, they must be close by' he thought to himself. Moses then turned and went in the opposite direction of the helicopter, he kept down low and close to trees so no one could spot him from the sky, Moses stood next to a tree waiting for the sound of the helicopter to go away just then he spotted a ground-unit of the Janoesian Army searching the woods twenty feet away from him. Moses went to make his way behind a large stone structure when someone called out to him "HEY YOU FREEZE" the voice ordered him, Moses turned around to see two soldiers behind him holding machine-guns, Moses dove behind the stone structure as the soldiers unloaded gunfire at him but missing him and hitting the stone structure. Moses stood up behind the stone structure and ran off into the bushes with the two soldiers giving chase, as he ran and tried to keep low bullets were whizzing past his head and lodging into tree trunks around him. Moses ran and ended up along a cliff side now realizing that he was boxed in his heart was pumping rapidly in his chest and he started changing into Silverback. The soldiers stopped their pursuit for Moses near the cliff side they knew that they had him boxed in "COME ON OUT THERE'S NOWHERE TO GO" they ordered him, right then Silverback leaped up in the air from the bush he was hiding behind as he landed he went into a ground-roll and sweep-kicked two soldiers off their feet two other soldiers fired with their guns at him but the bullets deflected off his shield. One of the soldiers radioed in for back-up and more soldiers came to their aid, as they approached the cliff side they spotted Silverback swinging through the trees and unloaded gunfire on him.

General Teal and Jessepi Montoya was studying the map under the canopy trying to come up with a plan of action when Lieutenant Janes interrupted then "sir we've got him, he's just east of us along a cliff side" the lieutenant informed General Teal "did they capture him" the general asked "no we're doing our best to box him in" Lieutenant Janes replied "okay lieutenant tell your men to do their best to force him back west, Jessepi you and your men get over there as quick as possible" the general ordered them "yes sir" Lieutenant Janes saluted General Teal and left. Jessepi headed back to the jeep.

After being release from the hospital Remni Claus's wife drove him home, Remni suffered a fractured collar-bone and a cracked knee-cap from the explosion at the Space Lab. The doctor gave him a pair of crutches to use but first the doctor advised him to get as much rest as possible for the next month or so, he told Remni that the best thing for him is to keep pressure off his shoulders and legs. Remni didn't live too far from the hospital it only took his wife ten minutes to get home, when they got home she helped Remni out of the car and to the front door. She then opened the front door and helped him inside to the living room where he laid on the sofa as she went back out to the car to get his work-bag. Remni was planning on putting in for a transfer from the Space Lab, him and his wife were planning on moving back to Brookshore as soon as he got better. He missed home and being close to his parents he also missed the commute on the Jae Rail to Alan's Landing. Truthfully Remni was concerned about the situation at the Space Lab and about the creature that escaped, it could be anywhere right now and Remni was worried about him and his wife's safety 'what if they can't capture it' he thought to himself.

"Alright boys it's game-time" Jessepi told Kelso and Bruno as he started up the jeep and peeled out from where he was, Kelso got his rifle ready while Bruno loaded his HS2000 handgun. Jessepi drove through the forest at a high rate of speed causing the jeep to bounce up and down when he drove over rocks and large branches that broke off of trees "keep your eyes focused up in the trees for this thing" he told his men. So Bruno and Kelso stared up in the trees trying to spot whatever they were looking for "what does this thing look like" Kelso asked Jessepi "like a giant gorilla" Jessepi replied. Just then Bruno spotted something large on the trunk of a Sabal palm-tree "what the fuck is that" he said as he stared at it, Jessepi stopped the jeep and turned around to see what Bruno was looking at "that's him" Jessepi told his men. They started unloading gunfire at Silverback but the bullets only bounced off his shield, Kelso got out of the jeep and aimed his rifle at Silverback before he could shoot Silverback lashed out his whip and with a crack of the whip knocked the rifle out of Kelso's hands. Kelso was shock at what he just experienced, he hid behind the jeep and grabbed his handgun and started shooting at it. Silverback jumped from one tree to another making it hard for Jessepi and his men to get a handle on him "where is he" Bruno asked the others "he's circling around us" Jessepi replied as he ran and hid behind a tree, he had his compound bow with him he aimed it at Silverback from behind the tree and shot an arrow that stuck into Silverback's right shoulder. Silverback started swinging through the trees again with the arrow still lodged in his shoulder trying to keep his distance from Jessepi and his men "where did he go" Kelso asked "don't worry he's not that far" Jessepi replied as he jumped back in the jeep "get in guys, let's go" he told his men. Jessepi drove through the forest in the direction that Silverback went "there's no getting away" Jessepi said to himself as he looked up in the trees while focusing on driving trying to spot the large gorilla. Kelso took a pair of binoculars out of his gear and stared up in the trees through them "do you see anything" Jessepi asked him "no nothing" Kelso replied "how did it get away from us" Bruno asked the other men. Silverback was sitting in a Gumbo limbo-tree he had just pulled the arrow out of his shoulder and was doing his best to keep hidden from Jessepi and his men. The wound the arrow made in his shoulder healed up within a few seconds only leaving a minor scar "cool" Silverback said to himself as he looked at the scar on his shoulder. Silverback wasn't out to kill these men but by the looks of it they were out to kill him so he had no choice, he stood up in the tree and started beaten his chest with his fist and let out a roar that was heard throughout the central Black Forest region. Jessepi heard the roar and stopped the jeep immediately "what the hell was that" Bruno said as he looked up into the trees "I think it's best that we split up we can cover more ground that way" Jessepi told his men, Kelso and Bruno got out of the jeep "okay Bruno you cover the southwest end and Kelso you cover the northeast side and I will stay central" Jessepi instructed his men, Kelso and Bruno started hiking into the woods "don't forget to keep your radios on" Jessepi told them as they left. As he hiked through the woods Bruno was holding a M4 Colt Commando assault rifle, he had never been to Janoesha Harbour before much less the Black Forest, he initially thought it would be similar to eastern Africa but the topography was all wrong. Bruno looked up into the trees but saw nothing just then he heard a whistling sound from behind him when he turned around to see what it was a steel shield had been hurled like a frisbee at him, it was coming at a great speed and force looking to cut him in half. Before that happened Bruno ducked under it rolled on the ground and hid behind a tree still holding his rifle, the shield sliced through the trunk of a palm-tree. "Holy shit" Bruno said to himself as he sat on the ground behind a tree, Bruno peeked out from behind the tree to see which direction was the shield thrown from. While Bruno was looking to see where the shield came from Silverback jumped out of the tree he was hiding behind and stuck his sword through the top of Bruno's head and into his neck, Bruno started twitching in shock as life left his body. Silverback then pulled the sword out, Bruno's body fell up against the tree, Silverback went and retrieved his shield from the other tree, Silverback also took Bruno's radio so he could keep tabs on what the soldiers were doing, he knew someone would be radioing in soon to check up on this guy. Jessepi drove his jeep through the Black Forest as he did so he looked up into the trees to see if he could spot where the large gorilla was but he saw nothing just blue skies and a whole lot of greenery. He radioed into his men to see where they were "I'm coming upon a river, no sign of the beast yet" Kelso replied "okay keep looking" Jessepi told him. Jessepi was concerned about Bruno he never got any reply from him so he tried again "B come in what is your position, B where are you" still no reply "shit" Jessepi said to himself as he put his radio on the front passenger seat.

Maureen took a taxi home from the hospital because her husband was out of town on a work assignment and he took the car with him, her left arm was casted and in a sling, the taxi pulled up the drive way of her house she paid the driver and got out, the driver helped bring her bags to the front door. "Thank you" she said to him as he put them down and left, she opened up the front door and went in she left her bags just inside the front door beside a shoe-rack. Maureen sat down it the living room and turned on the TV, there was a news bulletin on the TV, breaking news out at the Black Forest the Janoesian Army was looking for something out there. On the news they showed wounded soldiers on stretchers being loaded into army medical vans, Maureen could see that it didn't look good "oh my God what's happening there" she said to herself as she turned up the volume on the TV. Standing in front of a Channel 8 news van was General Teal standing next to him was Janet Jacobson for TJNX news she had a news microphone in her hand "coming live from the Black Forest this is Janet Jacobson with TJNX news, I'm here with Robert Teal a general in the Janoesian Army, Mr. Teal are there any new developments here at the Black Forest" she asked General Teal as she put the microphone up to his mouth "at this moment we haven't found what we're looking for but we do have it surrounded and I'm confident that it will be captured soon" he informed Janet "I was informed that a few of your soldiers were killed while hunting this thing" she asked the general "we anticipate these set-backs and are confident that we'll have this situation wrapped up before the sun goes down" he assured her. "What is it that you're hunting" Janet asked General Teal "I'm not at liberty to say" he replied "can you tell us if this is related to what happened at the Space Lab" she asked him "yes I believe so" he replied "okay that's it for the questions" General Teal said and left. Maureen changed the channel "what are they hiding" she said to herself, she stretched her legs out on the couch as she started watching Wheel Of Fortune. Before leaving the hospital the doctor had prescribed her pain-killers for her arm and the pain she felt in her back, Maureen was contemplating if she still wanted to work at the Space Lab. It's a good thing that she didn't have to go back to work right away, this gave her time to think about what she wanted to do. Truth was for about a year and a half Maureen had been thinking about getting a job at the zoo in Alan's Landing the Space Lab was becoming too political since the army bought into it plus she needed employment that was less strenuous on her.

Stacey and Shelby had been hiking for awhile, five minutes back they had pasted a stone silo but decided not to check it out "maybe we should have seen what was in that silo" Shelby said to Stacey "there was probably wild animals living in there didn't you see the windows were busted out" Stacey told her. They came upon an open field of tall grass surround by African oil palm-trees, before entering the field they stopped and hid behind a tree "what's going on" Shelby asked Stacey "take a look" Stacey replied as she motioned towards the field. Shelby took a look, in the field there was a group of soldiers holding machine-guns walking beside a tank patrolling the area "what are we going to do, there's nowhere to go" Shelby asked "we're going to wait here until they're gone" Stacey replied. As they hid behind the tree waiting for the soldiers to leave they could hear gunfire nearby "I'm scared Stacey" Shelby said as she cuddled up next to the tree (if there was a hole in the tree big enough for her to hide in she probably would have) "don't worry nobody knows we're here" Stacey assured her. The soldiers had finished their patrol of the area and were gone, Stacey peeked out from behind the tree and saw no one in the field "okay the coast is clear now" she told Shelby. They got up from where they were hiding and started hiking again through the field, Stacey took the hand-gun out of her backpack and held it in her hand just to feel safe. In the field the sun was hot as now they could see the open sky. As they made it to the other end of the field Stacey raised her gun ready to shoot just in case someone jumps out from behind a tree, especially a soldier "I wonder how close those gun shots were" Shelby asked her "hopefully not too close" Stacey replied. The forest was thick with bushes, vines and trees, there was no more beaten path for them to walk on the ground was rugged with rock, dirt and old decaying branches that broke off of trees. Stacey and Shelby did their best to hike through the forest as they stepped over logs and large rocks, Shelby was behind Stacey looking around cautiously, she kept hearing sounds of wild animals around her, as she looked up in the trees she saw Spider monkeys swinging from branches. Stacey stopped suddenly again "what's wrong now" Shelby asked her, Stacey pointed in front of her, in the distance there was another open area that had a channel 8 news van in it along with a canopy and a bunch of soldiers. Stacey recognized the lady standing beside the news van it was Janet Jacobson "it looks like this is where the army setup their base" Stacey said to Shelby "maybe Janet can help us" Shelby said to Stacey "no it's too risky" Stacey told her. They stood in the forest behind a large banyan tree shielding themselves from the view of the soldiers "so where do we go from here" Shelby asked Stacey feeling like they were trapped "I'm not too sure I'll figure something out" Stacey replied. Just then two soldiers holding machine-guns came up behind them "hands up" one of the soldiers ordered them, the two women were surprised and were cot off guard, Stacey and Shelby raised their arms up, the soldiers could see that Stacey was holding a hand-gun so they took it off her "lets go" one of the soldiers instructed them, the soldiers took them into their base.

Kelso was on the banks of the Sambar Horn River he just got off the radio with Jessepi and was now searching the bank of the river, he was holding an assault rifle attached to a sling that was around his neck heading down river as he headed down river he occasionally looked up in the trees that grew along the river bank. "Come on motherfucker show yourself" Kelso said as he looked up in the trees, just then he saw something perched up in large mahogany-tree on the otherside of the river, he did a double-take as he thought he missed it, when he looked again it was clear to him it was the beast. Kelso raised his rifle and let off a couple rounds in the direction of

Silverback, Silverback put his shield up in front of him to deflect the bullets "fuck" Kelso said to himself and then started running down river. Silverback swung through the trees following Kelso down the river, while Kelso was running he looked up into the trees across the river and saw Silverback following him. Silverback then threw his sword at Kelso the sword sliced across Kelso's right bicep and stuck in a tree stump next to him, Kelso grimaced in pain as his arm went limp but he kept running down river. He hid behind a large rock and looked at his arm, the wound wasn't too bad but it did need to be stitched up, Kelso took out a medic-kit from the small pack he wore around his waist in the medic-kit he took out some ointment and dripped it on his wound (it burned a little) he the took out a plastic see-through band-aid and stuck it on the wound. Kelso closed the medic-kit and started looking around to see where Silverback was, he didn't see anything so he got to his feet from behind the rock, just then he heard a loud roar he looked to where the sound was coming from and saw Silverback perched on the trunk of a tree about twenty feet away from him. Kelso raised his rifle to shoot but before he could do so Silverback threw his shield like a frisbee and cut off Kelso's right arm, Kelso screamed out in pain as his severed arm fell to the ground. With his other hand he took his bowie knife out of its sheath to defend himself as he did so

Silverback leaped off the tree trunk while holding his sword and cut off his head. Kelso's headless body collapsed to the ground as blood squirted out of his neck.

THE DUEL

Stacey and Shelby were brought to the canopy where General Teal was "sir we found these two hiding in the bushes" one of the soldiers told General Teal as they entered under the canopy. "Isn't this a surprise it's Stacey Lane, welcome Miss Lane we've been looking for you" General Teal said "what's going on here" Stacey asked the general "we're doing a routine sweep of the Black Forest" General Teal replied "what are you looking for" Stacey inquired "it's a training program" the general replied "looks more like you're hunting something" Stacey said "very perceptive Miss Lane" the general said. The two soldiers sat Stacey and

Shelby down in two fold-out chairs that was under the canopy they stood guard behind them "what are you planning to do with us" Shelby asked the general "right now I'm not too sure but what I need to know is if Miss Lane made a copy of the flash-drive she stole from us" General Teal said. "All this is for a flash-drive" Shelby asked the general, General Teal ignored Shelby's question and started looking at the map on the table "why don't you tell her what you're really doing here" Stacey said to the general "and what are we doing here Miss Lane" General Teal asked Stacey looking up from his map at her "you're hunting for Moses" Stacey replied "yes and we will find him" he told her as he walked over and stood in front of her "no you won't, he know this forest like the back of his hand" Stacey told the general "so do I Miss Lane so do I" he replied. General Teal looked at both Stacey and Shelby and then at the two soldiers standing behind them "take them to the trailer make sure you handcuff their hands together and stay there with them" he ordered the soldiers "yes sir" the soldiers complied.

Jessepi radioed in to his men to get their position but got no response, he had parked his jeep and was now on foot holding a SAR 80 assault rifle with a sling attached to it that was around his neck "hello if you guys are out there report back" he said into the radio and then hooked it back onto his belt. Jessepi cautiously hiked through the woods looking up into the trees for any signs of Silverback, just then he heard over his radio a deep amplified voice "your men are dead and you're next" the voice said. Jessepi now realized that it was up to him to take this thing down so he got back on his radio "here I am come and get me ape" Jessepi said calling Silverback out, he made sure he had a few stun-grenades on him but he did leave his compound bow in the jeep. As he was hiking Jessepi had his assault rifle up and ready for action, he then heard a loud roar and looked up into the trees and saw nothing, with his rifle pointed up in the trees he was ready to shoot at anything bigger than a bird. Just then Silverback rolled along the ground at a great rate of speed knocking Jessepi flying like a bowling-pin, Jessepi landed in a patch of bushes and then got to his knees and immediately started firing at Silverback but the bullets just deflected off Silverback's shield as Silverback came running towards him. Jessepi then took a stun-grenade pulled the pin and threw it at Silverback, it went off in front of him causing Silverback to tumble backwards and temporary impairing his vision, Jessepi got to his feet and started firing at him again bullets hit Silverback in the chest and shoulders as he wipe his eyes with his forearm. The bullets didn't kill him but they did draw blood and slow him down until he got his sight back and then jumped up into a tree while shielding himself from any additional bullets "GET BACK HERE ANIMAL" Jessepi screamed at him as he shot at him blindly in the tree. Jessepi went back to his jeep to get his compound bow and his Kopis sword, he put the sword in the sheath he wore behind his back and carried the bow in his hand. Jessepi had a collection of steel-tip arrows that he also wore behind his back, as he started hiking again he looked up in the trees "I KNOW YOU'RE HERE SHOW YOURSELF" he called out to Silverback. Just then Silverback leaped out of a tree holding his sword over his head in a chopping motion as he came down towards Jessepi, Jessepi pulled out his sword and blocked Silverback's sword, the weight of Silverback brought Jessepi to his knees as he held his sword over his head preventing Silverback from wounding him. Jessepi rolled out of the way of Silverback's sword and got to his feet, he put his bow up against a Sabal palm tree and started walking towards Silverback with his sword raised up in front of him "time to die ape" he told Silverback. They rushed towards each other with their swords, when their swords connected (steel meeting steel) it sent off sparks, they fought in the woods like two fencing champions, this lasted for close to twenty minutes until Silverback kicked Jessepi and sent him flying up against a tree. Jessepi's unconscious body slid down the tree's trunk and landed in a brier patch, Silverback thought he was dead and left in the opposite direction.

General Teal was still under the canopy studying the map of the Black Forest he hoped Jessepi made some headway in capturing Silverback. He really wanted the beast captured so he could take him back to Base Laysan for research, the whole idea was to draw a strain of his blood to extract DNA so they could create more soldiers like him. He also was thinking what he should do with Miss Lane and her friend they had seen too much to be released, he also needed to know if she made any copies of the flash-drive and if so find out where they were before he could kill them. Lieutenant Janes came back to the canopy with a cell-phone in his hand "sir there's a doctor from Base Laysan on the phone for you" the lieutenant informed him "thank you" he said to Lieutenant Janes as he took the phone from him "give me five minutes" he told the lieutenant "yes sir" Lieutenant Janes replied and then left. "General Teal" he said into the phone, a doctor at the hospital in Base Laysan informed him that General Banes just woke up out of his coma a few seconds ago but would need to stay in the hospital a few more days for neural testing "thank you doc" he said and then hung up the phone. That was good news for General Teal that Terrance was going to be okay, it was such a relief he didn't want to lose Terrance he was too much of a good friend and when all this is over maybe they could sit down and have a few drinks together. Lieutenant Janes came back to retrieve the cell-phone "lieutenant can you roll up this map for me and take it to my Humvee I'll be in the trailer" he told Lieutenant Janes "yes sir" the lieutenant replied.

Jessepi woke up feeling dizzy, holding and shaking his head trying to get back to his senses, when his head cleared he realized that he was sitting in a brier patch the front of his shirt had rips in it from the brier's thorns. He got to his feet and bushed himself off, picked up his sword that was laying on the ground and started looking for Silverback "I'm gonna kill that ape" he said to himself as he realized that his forearms were bleeding with minor wounds caused by the brier patch. Jessepi grabbed his bow from up against the Sabal tree and then headed back to his jeep as he hiked back to his jeep he didn't realize that he was being stocked by two female jaguars until he spotted one of them with the corner of his eye hiding behind a Walking palm. Jessepi got his bow and arrow ready, aimed it at the wild cat and shot, the arrow stuck in the neck of the jaguar as it tumbled over on the ground dead, the other cat leaped out from behind some bushes at Jessepi, Jessepi took out his sword and chopped off its head, the headless jaguar's body landed on the ground with blood gushing out from its severed neck. Jessepi got back to his jeep he put his bow and sword on the front passenger seat he took a Sig Sauer 9mm hand gun from the jeep's glove-compartment, he checked if it was loaded and it was. General Teal had put it there for him to use sort of like an additional present along with the jeep, Jessepi put it on the dashboard just in case he saw that ape while he was driving. Jessepi started up the jeep and started driving through the forest again, he looked up in the trees as the jeep bounced up and down the rugged terrain of the forest. He heard a loud roar and stopped the jeep, he grabbed the handgun off the dashboard as he looked up in the trees "where are you" he said to himself as he cocked the gun aiming it up into the trees. Just then a steel battle shield came hurling through the air like a buzz-saw and sliced through the hood of the jeep and into its motor totally disabling the jeep. White smoke started coming out of the damaged motor, Jessepi started shooting in the direction of where the shield came from but it was only blind-shooting he didn't see anything. He gathered up his gear and got out of his jeep, from here on he was going to be on foot, Jessepi put the handgun in his backpack and hoisted the backpack over his shoulder he then grabbed his assault rifle and started jogging. He did a short jog to a large banyan tree where he hid his backpack, he put his sword back in its sheath and took the handgun out of the backpack and tucked it in his belt around his waist he then grabbed his assault rifle and went looking for Silverback "this time you're dead ape" he said to himself as he jogged through the forest.

Stacey and Shelby was sitting on wooden chairs in a mobile trailer the Janoesian Army brought to the Black Forest, they had their hands cuffed behind their backs with a soldier watching over them. Stacey looked at Shelby "are you alright" Stacey asked her "what are they going to do with us" Shelby asked her in a concerned voice "I'm sorry I got you into this" Stacey said to her. General Teal entered into the trailer "how you doing ladies" he asked Stacey and Shelby, they gave him no answer "you can go now private and keep post outside" General Teal told the soldier watching over them "yes sir" the soldier replied and left the trailer. "So I've been thinking what to do with you ladies" the general said to Stacey and Shelby "your boyfriend is very lucky that General Banes didn't die in that explosion" he added as he looked at Stacey. "You're not going to get away with this" Stacey told him "we're the army you have no idea what we're able to getaway with" the general replied "if it were up to General Banes you two would be put in front of a firing-squad" he told the two women "but that's too barbaric, I'm a civil man I have a better plan for you two" he said while giving them a devious smile. This really worried Shelby, she was doing her best not to show any emotions but General

Teal saw that she was worried "don't worry all Miss Lane has to do is tell me where the other copies of the flash-drive are and this all goes away" he said to Shelby. "I advised them at the news station that if anything went wrong with me that they should send a copy of the flash-drive to Public Announcement Corp" Stacey informed General Teal "I hope for your sake you didn't do something that dumb" the general said to her.

Jessepi spotted Silverback perched on a large tree-branch, Jessepi stopped and looked at him as he raised his rifle to shoot, Silverback was staring back at Jessepi as he held his battle-shield. Jessepi let off a couple rounds from his rifle but the bullets deflected off the battle-shield Silverback held in front of him. Silverback let out a roar and leaped off the tree's branch into the air while he pulled his sword out of its sheath bringing it down towards Jessepi's head, before he could connect Jessepi jumped out of the way and pulled out his handgun letting off a few shots, this time the bullets hit Silverback in the shoulder creating deep wounds. Jessepi could see that the wounds caused by his bullets were healing rapidly and just left a scar "WHAT THE FUCK" Jessepi shouted as he raised his rifle and started shooting at Silverback "WHAT KIND OF MONSTER ARE YOU" he asked Silverback as he continued shooting, the bullets deflected off Silverback's shield. Silverback grabbed his whip from around his neck whipped it out towards Jessepi and with a snap! It wrapped tightly around the barrel of Jessepi's rifle giving Silverback the opportunity to yank the gun out of Jessepi's hands. The rifle came flying backwards towards Silverback, Silverback cot it and started firing at Jessepi, Jessepi ran for cover behind a Strangler fig-tree, behind the tree Jessepi took a stun-grenade and tossed it over by Silverback, it went off causing Silverback to tumble backwards while shielding his eyes with his forearm. This gave Jessepi enough time to take up position behind a naseberry bush, he got out his bow and took an arrow from behind his back and aimed it at Silverback. Silverback was just getting to his feet after being stunned by the grenade when a arrow pierced into his chest right above his heart, Silverback let out a loud roar and pulled the arrow out of his chest, the open wound healed up to where it was only a scar "fuck" Jessepi said from behind the bush. Silverback broke the arrow with one hand and tossed it aside he then picked up Jessepi's rifle and snapped it in two over his knee and left it there for Jessepi while he took off into the woods. Jessepi came out from behind the bushes and went over to where his rifle was laying 'it's going to be hard to kill this thing' he thought to himself as he looked at his broken rifle 'especially if he can heal rapidly like that'. Jessepi retrieved his backpack from the banyan tree and started hiking again, he got on his radio and radioed into General Teal's frequency "general I can't kill it I'm going to have to capture it some how" he informed the general. As he hiked through the woods, Jessepi was thinking of ways on how to capture Silverback 'maybe a booby-trap will work' he thought to himself "it would be good to have some rope" he said 'but then there's plenty of vine around' he thought into it. He had a plan he would make a Punji Sticks type trap, he remembered that he had a entrenching tool in his backpack, this he used to dig a hole about six feet deep after that he sharpened pieces of bamboo with his fixation Bowie-knife into sharp daggers, with a vine he tied them to broken tree branches then stuck the branches in the soft clay that was at the bottom of the hole he dug so the bamboo daggers stood up straight while the clay was drying. As the clay dried Jessepi urinated on the daggers he then sat beside the hole platting three long pieces of vine together to make a rope and knotted both ends, he rolled up the rope and put it around his neck. Jessepi covered up the hole with branches and dry leaves, his plan was to lower Silverback to this area so he would fall into the hole. Jessepi marked the area on the trunk of a tree with his Bowie-knife and started hiking again, on his hike he came upon two soldiers that were patrolling the area "how you guys doing" he asked the soldiers. The soldiers recognized Jessepi they seen him earlier talking with General Teal "not too bad" one of the soldiers replied "Jessepi Montoya" he said as he shook their hands "Sergeant Briggs and this is First Sergeant Cole" Briggs said introducing himself. "Have you saw or heard anything out here recently" Jessepi asked the two soldiers "no just a loud roar earlier" Cole replied "I believe the creature is still in this area" Jessepi told them "how do you know that" Briggs asked him "because I was fighting with him not too long ago" Jessepi replied. First Sergeant Cole remembered that he seen Jessepi with two other men earlier driving in a jeep "wasn't it three of you that came here" Cole asked him "yeah now it's only me" Jessepi replied "if you need any help we're here for you" Briggs told him. "Yes you guys can help me" Jessepi told them "okay" Briggs replied with some intrigued in his voice "I made a trap about thirty yards back and I need someone to lower the creature there, soon as it's trapped I can take it from there" Jessepi told the two soldiers. Just then the three men heard a loud roar and looked up in the trees they saw Silverback sitting in a oak tree over thirty feet above them, Cole and Briggs aimed their machine-guns towards him and started shoot. Silverback threw his battle shield like a frisbee the shield hurled through the air like a giant buzz-saw at the men, Cole and Jessepi jumped out of its path but it sliced Sergeant Briggs in two, Briggs's body collapsed to the ground in a pool of his own blood. Jessepi looked up into the oak tree and saw Silverback coming down the trunk of the tree, Jessepi got to his feet and started running to where his trap was Cole followed behind him, Silverback saw the two men running and chased after them. When Jessepi got to where his trap was he jumped over the camouflaged hole and hid behind a nearby tree Cole was behind him running with Silverback on his tail, Cole looked behind him and started shooting at Silverback as he was running. Silverback was just about to leap at him when Cole fell into Jessepi's trap, Cole screamed out in pain as he was impaled on the bamboo daggers he laid there at the bottom of the hole slowly dying. Jessepi peeked out from behind the tree he was hiding and saw nothing he waited a little while before coming out and checking the hole, when he did so he saw that it was First Sergeant Cole laying dead in the hole "fuck" he said to himself. Jessepi looked around to see if Silverback was nearby but he didn't see him, then Jessepi thought that maybe Silverback was in a tree watching him build the trap Jessepi started laughing "motherfucker" he said to himself.

General Teal's CB Radio that he wears hooked to his belt around his waist went off, it was Jessepi letting him know that he was going to capture Silverback instead of killing him. Jessepi informed the general that Silverback's body had a rapid healing process "thank you" General Teal said to Jessepi and turned off the radio "well it won't be too long until your boyfriend is captured" the general told Stacey. General Teal pulled up a chair and sat facing the two ladies, he looked at Stacey "I know you're lying about the news station, my men searched that station in and out two times and found nothing" the general told her "we also searched where your camera-man lives what was his name, Sedrick by the way he's no longer with us" General Teal told Stacey as he smirked at her. Stacey stared blankly at the general but inside she was boiling over with anger, General Teal stared back at her and then leaned back in his chair "I don't think you can keep this facade up very much longer" the general told her, Stacey smirked back at him "what are you planning on doing with us" she asked him "well in an hour you will be transported to Greystone" he replied "on what charge" Stacey inquired "domestic espionage" General Teal replied "that charge carries a twenty year sentence" the general informed her "but it doesn't have to be that way just tell me where the other copies are and this all goes away" he assured her. Stacey knew she couldn't tell him she knew he was bluffing about prison, he couldn't afford for her to go to court that is how she knew if she told him where the copy was she and Shelby wouldn't make it to court, this is all the leverage she has, plus she didn't make any copies "guess I'm just going to have to try my luck in court" Stacey told the general. General Teal's eyes slightly opened wide shocked at what Stacey said to him "so you want to play games I'm the wrong person to play with sister" he said to her as he looked at her in disdain. He got up from his chair and went to the door of the trailer "I'll give you ladies some time to think about it" he told them as he left through the door, the soldier standing guard outside came back into the trailer to watch over Stacey and Shelby.

Jessepi left Cole's body in the hole and started hiking again there wasn't much he could do, carrying Cole's body over his shoulder would just slow him down. On his hike he came upon the Sambar Horn River, he went down to the river's bank and stooped down in front of its slow flowing clear-blue water and filled his canteen. As Jessepi was filling his canteen he looked to his left and saw a body laying next to some bushes about forty feet away from where he was, after filling his canteen he went over to check it out. As he got closer he could see by the boots the body was wearing that it was Kelso, Jessepi ran over to check if he was still alive but when he got there he could see that he wasn't (the body was headless). Where was his head, Jessepi looked around but didn't see it 'had Silverback kept it as a souvenir' he thought to himself. Jessepi knelt down beside Kelso's body and said a prayer for him before he started back on his hike "you were a great soldier comrade may peace be with you as I settle this score" he said to the headless body. Jessepi got to his feet and started hiking again, he hiked along the bank of the river hoping to run into Silverback or find Kelso's head. Along the river bank Jessepi came upon a large tree stump from an oak tree the stump was hollowed out so someone or something could sit or live inside it. Jessepi sat inside it and rested for awhile drinking out of his canteen, he took some energy bars out of his backpack and started munching on them, as he was finishing off his last energy bar he heard a loud roar, Jessepi immediately got out of the tree stump with his assault rifle ready to shoot at anything threatening. He looked around up in the trees and saw nothing "come on I know you're here" he said to himself, he turned around and looked into the woods behind him that's when he saw Silverback running towards him. Jessepi started firing at Silverback but kept missing him because Silverback was deking in between and around trees preventing Jessepi from having a stationery target. As Silverback got closer he took out his sword, Jessepi started running along the bank of the river trying to keep his distance Silverback saw him and gave chase. As Jessepi was running he looked to see where Silverback was and saw him in the woods chasing after him, he took a stun-grenade out of his pack, pulled the pin and tossed it over to where Silverback but Silverback saw it coming and deked around it as it went off. Jessepi then hid behind a large rock and took out his bow and arrow as Silverback came charging towards him behind the rock Jessepi stood up and shot the arrow hitting Silverback in the stomach while he leaped at Jessepi. The arrow pierced deep into Silverback's stomach as he landed in the water, Silverback splashed about as the current carried him down the river. Jessepi stood there watching as Silverback floated down river, he didn't know how far down the river went so he decided on go back to General Teal and asking him.

Silverback grabbed onto a large rock that was protruding out of the water and climbed up an sat on it, he pulled the arrow out of his stomach and sat there watching his stomach heal into a scar. He hadn't went too far down river, he knew Jessepi would be heading back to General Teal to find out how far the river went because he had listen to them on the radio in conversation. Silverback jumped off the rock onto the trunk of a tree he then started swinging through the trees to where General Teal setup base.

Stacey and Shelby were in the trailer wondering what General Teal would do next, Stacey turned to the soldier watching over them "can we get something to eat we're hungry" she asked him "not until the general comes back" he replied "well can we at lease get something to drink we're about to pass out from dehydration" Stacey inquired "I'll see what I can do" the soldier replied. The soldier took two handcuffs and handcuffs both lady's right ankle to the foot of the metal table that was in front of them, he then left the trailer and locked the door behind him. "What are you up to" Shelby curiously asked Stacey "just trying to buy us some time" Stacey replied "time for what our feet and hands are handcuffed" Shelby inquired "I just needed us alone for awhile" Stacey told her "why" Shelby asked her "we need to try to escape that's the only chance we have to stay alive" Stacey informed her "okay so what's your plan" Shelby asked her. "When the soldier comes back he's going to take the handcuffs off from around our ankles then he's going to have to free one of our hand so we can drink and that will be our chance to escape" Stacey told her "what do you want me to do" Shelby asked her "just follow my lead" Stacey told her.

It didn't take Jessepi that long to get back to base-camp, he met with General Teal under the canopy "so how's the hunt going" General Teal asked him "that's why I can back, Silverback fell in the river and it took him down stream how far down stream I don't know so I need to know how far south does that river go" Jessepi asked the general "what river are you talking about" General Teal asked him "it's very wide about a twenty minute hike west of here" Jessepi replied. "Oh the Sambar Horn River it goes all the way south just north of Alan's Landing" the general informed him "then I need a vehicle so I can patrol along that river" Jessepi told him "what's wrong with your jeep" General Teal asked him "it's out of commission" Jessepi replied. General Teal reached into his pants pocket and took out four set of keys "okay take one of the humvees" he told Jessepi as he handed him a key. Jessepi took the key and headed for the closest humvee which was an NXT360 Humvee, he opened the door and got in the driver's seat. He stuck the key in the ignition and started it up the engine purred like a cat getting its belly rubbed, Jessepi drove towards the Sambar Horn River.

Silverback was hungry so he sat in a banana-tree eating bananas and letting the peels fall to the ground, a group of spider-monkeys were sitting with him in the tree. After eating a few bananas Silverback started swinging through the trees again heading to where General Teal setup camp. It didn't take him too long to get to his destination, he sat in a Sabal palm tree looking down on the base the Janoesian Army setup in the Black Forest. He recognized a three star general standing beside a humvee the general left and went under a canopy 'that looks like General Teal' he thought to himself. Silverback sat there trying to figure out a plan of attack 'I guess the only way is to go in there and clean house' he thought to himself. Silverback threw his battle shield like a frisbee it sliced through a humvee killing the two soldiers inside and lodged into a large mahogany tree trunk. Other soldiers saw the shield cut through the humvee and started firing their machine guns up in the trees but it was only panic-fire they didn't see anything. General Teal came out from under the canopy "WHAT'S GOING ON" he called over to Lieutenant Janes ducking behind a humvee "I THINK WE'RE BEING ATTACKED SIR" Lieutenant Janes shouted to the general as he hid behind the humvee. General Teal attempted to run to his humvee that when Silverback jumped out of the tree with his sword drawn he landed on the general humvee caving in the roof of it and piercing his sword through the hood destroying the humvee's engine. Silverback stood there on the humvee looking at the general with rage in his eyes, General Teal was surprised to see Silverback a bunch of soldiers started firing their guns at Silverback but he deflected the bullets with his sword, his eyes never left the general "time to die general" he said to General Teal. Just then a soldier launched a rocket from a bazooka at Silverback, the rocket hit the front of the humvee and blew-up the force of the explosion hurled Silverback up against a tree twenty feet away. This gave General Teal the opportunity to make a ran for the trailer, so he did, when he got to the trailer he locked himself in. Silverback got up off the ground he shook his head clearing away the dizzy feeling, a group of soldiers were moving in closer to him so he rolled on the ground at a great rate of speed and bowled them over like a wrecking-ball the soldiers flew through the air like dummies and slammed into trees causing their bones to break. Silverback retrieved his shield from out of the tree's trunk and started looking for where General Teal went, Lieutenant Janes grabbed an AR-15 machine gun from out of the humvee he was hiding behind and started shooting at Silverback but the bullets were deflecting off Silverback's shield. Silverback took the whip from around his neck whipped it out and with a snap! It wrapped around the lieutenant's gun and Silverback yanked it out of his hand, Lieutenant Janes stood there shocked, Silverback then threw his shield like a frisbee and cut off the lieutenant's head. Lieutenant Janes body collapsed to the ground with blood gushing out of its severed neck, the shield came back around to Silverback like a boomerang. Silverback was still being shot at by soldiers so he let his shield protect him, he was too busy trying to figure out where General Teal went 'he was most likely hiding somewhere' Silverback thought, but where. Silverback then looked to his left and saw a trailer about forty feet away under a cluster of palm trees and bushes so as he sliced his way through a bunch of soldiers he went to check out the trailer.

General Teal entered into the trailer and locked the door behind him, he noticed that Stacey and Shelby were the only ones in the trailer "where did that soldier go that was here" he asked the two ladies "he went to get us something to drink we're real thirsty" Stacey replied. General Teal pulled out a Sig Sauer 9mm handgun from the holster that he wore around his waist "what's that for" Shelby asked him concerned for her safety "insurance" he replied and then stooped down behind Stacey's chair and put one of his arms around her shoulders and the gun to her temple. "No please don't" Shelby begged as she stared at him, just then they heard a loud thud sound on the roof of the trailer, the general and Shelby both looked up "what was that" Shelby said "I HAVE YOUR GIRLFRIEND HERE IF YOU DO ANYTHING I WILL KILL HER" General Teal shouted up to the roof. For a minute there was silence then the lights went out in the trailer that's when Stacey snapped her head back hitting the general in the nose and breaking it. General Teal instinctively dropped his gun and held his nose as blood started dripping from it, the gun landed on the floor in front of Shelby so she kicked it and it slid to the other side of the trailer. "Fucking bitch" General Teal called Stacey as he grabbed her hair and pulled her head back "I'm gonna cut your throat bitch" he told her, he reached for his Karambit knife that he had tucked in his belt around his waist just then the window in the trailer shattered. General Teal went to retrieve his gun but before he could pick it up off the floor Silverback threw his sword in through the open window and cut off the general's arm the general screamed out in pain as he held what was left of his right arm. He sat on the floor with his back braced up against a metal filing cabinet moaning in pain as beads of sweat started to form on his forehead. Silverback jumped in through the large open window he saw General Teal sitting on the floor and his sword stuck in the wall beside him "Moses" he heard a voice call to him and turned around to see Stacey and another lady handcuffed. Silverback went to retrieve his sword out of the wall "you won't get away you'll be hunted for the rest of your life" General Teal told him as he walked by him, Silverback swatted him across the face spraining his neck and knocking him out "shut up" Silverback told him as the general sat there unconscious. After he retrieved his sword Silverback went over to where Stacey and Shelby was and snapped open the handcuffs around their ankles and wrist. Stacey looked at Moses as she stood up "what did they do to you" she asked him "I guess this changes things now doesn't it" he said to her, she gave him a smile and then hugged him. "Oh this is my friend Shelby" Stacey said to Moses "okay we got to go more soldiers are coming" Moses informed them, Stacey and Shelby left through the door and

Silverback jumped out the window. When Stacey and Shelby got outside all they saw was bodies of dead soldier scattered all over the base, Stacey looked at Silverback "the general is right they're not going to stop hunting you" Stacey told him.

Jessepi drove the humvee down to the northwest section of Pearles, he parked on a old stone bridge and got out of the vehicle, he went to the edge of the bridge and looked over into the water below checking for any signs if Silverback exited the river. He radioed back to General Teal to let him know where he was and that he hasn't spotted Silverback yet but there was no response from the general "come in general I'm just southwest of Beryl Rado there's no sign of Silverback" he said into the radio "general are you there" Jessepi hooked the radio back on his belt. He had a feeling that something was wrong, perhaps he went too far down river with his search so he decided on heading back.

Stacey and Shelby had been hiking through the woods awhile with Silverback right behind them when they came upon a section of the Sambar Horn River. Stacey and Shelby went down to the river's bank and started drinking its clear-blue water, Silverback sat down behind them. Stacey looked behind her at Silverback sitting there "we're thirsty and tired we just need to rest a little" she told Silverback. Silverback didn't say anything he just looked at her he was happy to see that she wasn't hurt "oh by the way what did you do with the flash-drive I gave you" Stacey asked him "I gave it to a friend his sister works at the Orange Gate and she knows exactly what to do with it" he replied "so you didn't make any copies" she inquired "no just that one, don't worry it's in good hands" he assured her. Stacey and Shelby got their fill of water and stood up, Shelby was in aw as she stared at Silverback inside she was thanking her lucky stars that he was on their side. "We need to get back to highway 31 we hid Shelby's grey Sunfire off the road there" Stacey told him "it's going to be a hike, there's a clearing up ahead there's some jeeps there you can use to get to your car" Silverback informed them. Silverback picked up Stacey in his arms and Shelby climbed on his back an held on tight as he jumped over the river to the other side. They started hiking again, as Stacey and Shelby hiked through the woods Silverback picked a few mangoes off a Julie mango tree and gave them to the two women to eat. It took them about ten minutes to get to the clearing, before entering into the clearing the two women hid behind a large mahogany tree while Silverback climbed up a palm tree. In the clearing an army jeep was parked with three soldiers standing around it holding machine guns, Silverback threw his shield like a frisbee decapitating two soldiers the other soldier started shooting his gun up in the trees but hit nothing. He immediately got on his radio "I need some back up he's here hurry I need back up" he said into the radio in a desperate voice just then Silverback threw his sword into the soldier's chest, the force of the throw hurled the soldier backwards and pinned him up against a tree trunk, he hung there slowly dying. Silverback jumped out of the tree and picked up his shield then went and retrieved his sword "OKAY IT'S SAFE TO COME OUT" he called out to Stacey and Shelby. The two women came out from behind the mahogany tree, Silverback grabbed a set of keys out of the pants pocket of one of the headless soldiers laying on the ground. Stacey went over to where Silverback was while Shelby stood looking around for anymore soldiers, Silverback handed Stacey the set of keys "take that jeep to highway 31, there's a compass mounted on its dashboard so you won't get lost" he told Stacey "what are you going to do" Stacey asked him "I got one more thing to take care of" Silverback told her. "Okay lets go" Stacey told Shelby as she climbed into the jeep and sat behind the wheel, she started up the jeep as Shelby sat in the front passenger seat "be safe" Stacey said to Silverback as she drove away.

General Teal had woken up, he reached with his only hand for the radio that was hooked on his belt "Jessepi come in are you there don't come back to the base Silverback has killed everyone and is still at large" he said into the radio. Jessepi responded back "okay I copy, are you okay general" Jessepi asked General Teal "don't worry about me just report to Base Laysan" the general replied. General Teal slowly got to his feet as he used the filing cabinet as leverage, he took the scarf from around his neck and wrapped it around his severed arm, he moaned in pain as he wrapped the scarf around his arm. The door to the trailer had been left open so the general went outside when he got outside he stood looking at the carnage of bodies strewn all over the base. General Teal was looking for a vehicle but the only vehicle that looked operational was a jeep with a dead soldier behind the wheel. He went over to the jeep and saw that the keys were in the ignition so he pulled the body out of the driver's seat, the body fell to the ground with a thud and General Teal climbed into the jeep and started it up the gas meter indicated that it was half full so he drove off. 'It's not over yet ape' General Teal thought to himself as he drove through the Black Forest, he was planning on getting reinforcements and coming back for round two. As the general drove through the Black Forest he kept hearing movement from the trees above him but every time he looked up to see what it was he just saw birds so he ignored the sound and kept driving that's when a battle shield came hurling through the air and into the hood of the jeep destroying its motor bringing the jeep to a complete stop. General Teal went to check the glove-compartment for a hand-gun just then Silverback jumped in the seat behind him with his sword drawn and cut off the general's head, like a water-fountain blood squirted out of the general's severed neck the headless corpse fell out of the driver's seat onto the ground.

Frank Allister was at a restaurant in Base Laysan eating lunch he was going over some work papers from the stockpile when he over heard two lieutenants that were sitting at a table next to his talking about what was happening at the Black Forest. They mentioned the explosion at the Space Lab and that the army was hunting some large ape-like creature, they also mentioned Stacey Lane's name that's when Frank put aside his work papers to listen closer. They said General Teal had apprehended Stacey and another lady in the Black Forest, Frank knew that there was something wrong that Moses was in trouble so he decided on calling him on his cell-phone and got no answer it just went to his voice-mail so Frank left a message. Frank finished his lunch and got up from around the table as he put a ten dollar bill down for the waitress, he went outside and sat in his jeep that was parked in the parking lot of the restaurant he had fifteen minutes left on his lunch break. He sat there thinking about what the lieutenants were talking about and gave Moses a call again but still no answer so he decided on calling the TJNX News Station and asking for Stacey Lane the phone rang a couple times and then someone answered it was a Corporal Butler of the Janoesian Army "hi can I speak to a Stacey Lane please" Frank asked him "sorry she can't speak to you right now who's this calling" the corporal replied "that's okay I'll call back later" Frank told him and hung up. Frank was beginning to wonder if they had done something to Moses "I hope you're alright Mo" he said to himself as he started up his jeep. He backed out of the parking spot and turned right onto the main road, he headed back to work, Frank was planning on heading up to Tamerra after work.

CONNECTING THE PIECES

Stacey and Shelby got back to where they hid Shelby's car, Stacey parked the jeep on the shoulder of highway 31 and they both went to Shelby's car. When they got to the car they removed all the branches and leaves off of it, Shelby got in the driver's seat and Stacey in the front passenger seat, Shelby started up the car and drove off heading south on highway 31. "Where are we going" Shelby asked Stacey "let's head back to Tamerra" Stacey replied "what about Moses" Shelby asked her "he can handle himself plus he'll meet up with us there" Stacey told Shelby. Shelby turned right onto Route 23 "we got to get in contact with Frank

Allister he's the only one that can help Moses right now" Stacey said to Shelby. "How do we contact him" Shelby asked her "Moses has his number we'll go to his place I have an extra key" Stacey replied. Stacey was so worried for Moses she hoped that she could find a cure for him she also hoped that Frank could point her in the right direction, perhaps he knew where to go to find a cure.

Silverback was sitting in a Cempedak tree waiting to see if Jessepi would meet back up with General Teal, he had been sitting there for almost an hour when he decided on leaving 'maybe he ain't coming' he thought to himself. Silverback decided before his heart rate went down and he turned back into his normal self that he would head back to the Space Lab to find some answers. He stood up and started swinging through the trees at a hundred miles an hour, he stopped in a banana tree and ate a few bananas and then started swinging again. It didn't take him long to get to Tamerra he actually got there before Stacey and Shelby, Silverback sat in a tree behind the Space Lab watching soldiers patrol around the large building. 'They must have the Lab on lock down' he thought to himself, he saw that the wing where the explosion happened the army had covered with clear thick plastic. Silverback just sat there watch as men dressed in white jump-suits and mask collected paper and computers that had not been destroyed in the explosion 'shouldn't the JBI be on the scene collecting evidence, who are these guys' he thought to himself.

After work Frank called his wife at the hospital to let her know that he was heading up to Tamerra to meet Moses and that she would have to pick Maddy up from work. Madelline his daughter had graduated from high school last year and was working for a year before she headed off to university in Umni. Frank packed up his toolbox and put it in the back of his jeep and headed off base, when he got to the front gate of Base Laysan he signed out with a military police officer that was sitting in a booth "I should be a few hours" he informed the officer. The steel gate opened and Frank drove off, a mile down the road he entered onto Highway 32, Highway 32 was a pleasant highway to drive on one side of it overlooked the Atlantic Ocean and a beautiful view of sailboats sailing on its crystal-blue water. Frank wondered where the first place would be to look for Moses, he knew he was living on Route 55 not too far from Route 10, he didn't know which construction-site he was working at so he decided the best thing was to go where he lives. It took Frank just under an hour to get into downtown Tamerra, in Tamerra Highway 32 turned into Route 54 Frank had to make a left onto Route 55. He drove north on Route 55 until he got to Route 10, he parked on Route 10 in front of a parking-meter just outside of a Radisson hotel. Frank got out of the jeep and put two dollars in the meter, he went for a short walk along Route 55 until he seen Moses apartment building. He opened the front door to the building and went in there was a list of all the apartments on the wall to the right of him, on the list was the last names of the people that lived in the apartments. Frank saw Moses name he was on the top floor apartment 412 so Frank took the stairs up to the fourth floor. When he got to the fourth floor he looked for apartment 412 and found that it's door was slightly open, Frank was cautious on how he entered the apartment. He eased the door open with his hand "MO ARE YOU THERE" he called out as the door swung open but got no answer. He decided on entering in the apartment the apartment was a mess all the cupboards, cabinets and dressers had been opened up with paper scattered all over the floor and broken plates on the kitchen counter. To Frank it looked like someone was looking for something, but where was Moses, Frank looked around to find some evidence to directed him to where Moses was but found nothing. Frank stood there in the apartment thinking about the last conversation him and Moses had maybe there was a clue in there, then it dawned on him they were talking about the Primate Program. Frank knew that the Primate Program was happening at the Space Lab 'perhaps that's where Moses is' he thought to himself, Frank left the apartment and closed the door behind him. This time he took the elevator down to the lobby, Frank was going to checkout the Space Lab he was very concerned now 'was Moses in trouble' he thought to himself as he left the building and headed to his jeep. Frank got into his jeep and started it up he made a U-turn on Route 10 and drove off and headed east to Route 50.

Greg Olson is the Regional Commander for Edward Region he was at the hospital on Base Laysan he just finished visiting General Banes in the ICU. Now he was in the hospital's waiting room with his security talking on the phone with Ray Gatlain "yes I heard about the trouble at the Black Forest, I hope your man will be able to take care of the situation" he said to Ray "yes yes whatever he wants I can get him" Greg told Ray "how long? Okay I'll be here" Greg said and hung up the phone. Greg Olson had given General Banes the okay to start up the Primate Program without the President's knowledge and had endorsed $200,000 of the federal budget to spearhead the program, this was all done in secrecy at his home office.

Jessepi drove up to the front gate of Base Laysan the MP Officer in the booth came out and greeted him "how can I help you" the officer asked him "I'm here to see RC Elect Olson" Jessepi replied while showing the officer his driver's license. The officer took a look at his license and then opened the gate "he's at the hospital go straight and then make a right at the first street you can't miss it it's on your left" the officer told him. Jessepi entered into the base and followed the directions he was told, he hadn't seen a base this size before it was like it's own city (you really didn't have to leave the base if you lived here) Jessepi made the right turn. It didn't take him too long to get to the hospital, he parked the humvee outside the front lobby, got out and headed in the hospital, the waiting room was off to his right and front desk reception was to his left. He went up to the front desk there was a young lady in uniform sitting behind the desk "how can I help you sir" she asked him "I'm looking for RC Elect Olson" he replied, she pointed to the waiting room "he's over in the waiting room" she told him "thank you" he said to her as he left for the waiting room. Jessepi entered into the waiting room he saw a middle age man standing by the window wearing a dark grey two piece suit standing around him were a group of men also wearing suits and sunglasses. One of the men wearing sunglasses tapped Greg on the shoulder "sir I think he's here" he told Greg, Greg turned around from looking out the window to see Jessepi coming towards him. One of Greg's security stopped Jessepi before he got closer and patted him down for weapons, Jessepi had left all his weapons in the humvee, he raised his arms up and turned around so the man could pat him down. "He's clean" Greg's security told him, Greg motioned for Jessepi to come closer so he did. "Hi sir Jessepi Montoya" Jessepi said as he shook Greg's hand "Greg Olson" Greg replied "General Teal instructed me to talk with you" Jessepi informed him "yes I don't know if you're aware but we were just informed that they found General Teal's body beside a jeep in the Black Forest" Greg told him. Jessepi was surprise to hear that General Teal was dead "what happened" he asked Greg "apparently he had been decapitated" Greg replied "I'm willing to supply you with whatever you want but I have to know that you are able to capture this thing" Greg said to him "I am sir" Jessepi assured him. "There's one more thing I was told that a lady from the TJNX News Station stole a flash-drive from the Space Lab with some sensitive information on it, I need it back" Greg informed him "yes sir" Jessepi replied "this information cannot be released to the public" Greg told him and continued "now how can I help you" Greg asked him "I need a bazooka" Jessepi replied "sure I'll get that for you" Greg said. "Is that everything" Greg asked Jessepi "yes for now sir" Jessepi replied, Jessepi was thinking about the lady that stole the flash-drive "what's the lady's name that stole the flash-drive" he asked Greg "her name is Stacey Lane she's a thirty year old journalist for TJNX" Greg replied "what do you want me to do with her when I find the flash-drive" Jessepi inquired

"I think you know" Greg replied "yes sir" Jessepi said as he took a deep breath. They shook hands again and Jessepi left the hospital, as he got out front he was thinking about what he had to do, he had never killed a lady before, the thought of it really didn't sit well with him but it had to be done, Jessepi climbed into the humvee started it up and drove off.

Frank drove north on Route 50 to Route 4 where the Space Lab was located, the city limits pretty much stopped at Route 6 after that there was no more high-rise and commercial buildings just bungalows, trees, bushes and open meadows. As Frank drove north of Route 7 he could see the foothills to the Turynfoymus Mountains in the distance, this end of Route 50 had signs post cautioning motorist to be aware of wild animals crossing the road. As he crossed over Route 5 he saw the Space Lab on his left, he noticed that there was a few army humvees parked out on Route 50 in front of the Space Lab. The closer Frank got to the Space Lab he could see a couple government tagged cars parked across the street from the humvees. Frank turned left into the entrance of the Space Lab to talk with the guard at the gate, he pulled up beside the booth the guard was sitting in, the guard came out and greeted Frank "hi there how can I help you" he asked Frank "Staff Sergeant Frank Allister, what's going on here" Frank replied as he shook the guard's hand "the army is doing a internal investigation" the guard told him. "Can you open the gate please" Frank asked him, the guard looked at a list on a clipboard that he was holding in his other hand "sorry sir your name's not on the list" the guard replied "who's in charge here" Frank asked him "Lieutenant Gormann" the guard told him "can you let him know that Staff Sergeant Frank Allister wants to speak with him" Frank said "yes sir" the guard replied and went back into the booth. Frank watched as the guard got on his CB Radio he couldn't hear what he was saying, it only took five minutes and the guard came out of the booth and walked up to the jeep's driver's side window "okay you can go in, wait in the front lobby he'll be about twenty minutes take this visitor's card and clip it onto your shirt" the guard told him as he handed Frank the card. The guard went back into the booth and opened up the gate for Frank, Frank drove in and parked outside the front lobby of the Space Lab. He turned off the jeep's engine and sat there with the driver's side window open 'I wonder what they were investigating' Frank thought to himself, Frank heard about the explosion here it was all over the news 'but if it was just the explosion why would the army be here' Frank tried to make sense of it 'something more is happening here' he thought to himself.

Stacey and Shelby showed up outside Moses apartment, they were parked on Route 55 "stay here

I won't be long" Stacey told Shelby as she got out of the car. She went into the building's front door and took the elevator up to the fourth floor, Stacey walked down the hallway to Moses apartment, before she used her key she tried the door-knob, it wasn't unlocked so she slowly and cautiously opened the door "HELLO IS ANYBODY HERE" she called out as she stepped in but there was no answer. When she got in she closed the door behind her, she noticed that the place was a mess like someone was looking for something, every drawer in the apartment was pulled out and their contents were dumped on the floor. Stacey knew where Moses hid his phone-book so that's where she went to retrieve it, it was in his bedroom closet under a loose floor board, she knew whom ever was in here wouldn't find it only her and Moses knows where it is, no one would ever expect it to be under a floor board. Stacey knelt down in the closet flipping through Moses phone book for Frank's number she found it half way down the page towards the middle of the book, she put it in her contacts in her phone. After storing Frank's phone number in her phone she put the phone book back under the floor board and left the apartment, she made sure to lock the front door with her key.

After seeing what was going on at the Space Lab Silverback decided on heading back to the Black Forest, he found a good place he could stay for a while where he wouldn't get bothered by anyone. It was located in the western section of the Black Forest it's the highest peak of the Turynfoymus Mountain Range name Crest Climb. The ground up there was padded with peat moss with a few Lala palms and Wild Date palm trees around its surface. Silverback discovered a cave up there where he could take shelter if he ever needed to plus he was so high up he could see all of Tamerra from up there. As the sun went down over Janoesha Harbour Silverback sat there outside his cave looking down over Tamerra and its skyline, almost as if he were standing guard over the city. He sat there until the sun went completely down also until he fell asleep and turned back into his normal self.

Frank came out of his jeep and went into the front lobby of the Space Lab, two uniformed soldiers were sitting behind a desk to the right of him, he waved hi to them and they waved back. Frank took a seat on one of a group of black-leather stools that were lined up in front of a large display-like window, he sat there waiting for Lieutenant Gormann for what seemed like an hour. It was getting dark now and Frank was thinking about heading back to Base Laysan before Karen went to bed just then he seen Lieutenant Gormann coming down the steps from the second floor. The lieutenant came over to where Frank was sitting "hi Staff Sergeant, Lieutenant

Gormann" he said as he shook Frank's hand "hi sir" Frank said as he stood up and saluted him "at ease sergeant" Lieutenant Gormann told him and continued "how can I help you" the lieutenant asked him. Frank thought about it and he figured that the discreet approach would be the best way to handle his inquirers "I'm looking for a friend of mine that's been missing since the explosion" Frank told the lieutenant "have you checked the hospital" Gormann asked him "yeah they don't know where he his" Frank replied "all injured persons in the explosion were brought to the hospital" Gormann informed him. Frank was fishing for information "he came here to see General Banes" Frank said and continued "perhaps I can speak with the general" Frank asked Gormann "General Banes is not here at the moment" Gormann told him "maybe you can tell me why my friend would be meeting the general here" Frank asked him "sergeant I don't know who your friend is and this conversation is over" Gormann said to him as he turned around to head back upstairs "is this something I should bring to the attention of the Defense Minister" Frank asked Gormann in a sarcastic tone. Gormann stopped and turned around to face Frank "go home sergeant or I'll have you arrested" he told Frank.

Milton Addler is a thirty-five year old single dad that manages a stationery store in downtown Tamerra, Addler's Office Supplies it's named. It's a family run business thats been around for a hundred years, Milton worked the front desk and looked after inventory. At this moment in time he was doing inventory on a shipment of laptops that just came in, he was clearing space on the shelves to put them. Milton's sister worked at the Orange Gate in the Health & Human Services, she usually came by the store on her lunch break to see how he was doing. One afternoon she came by with a cup of coffee and a bag of donuts she had bought for him, they sat at the front desk and talked awhile, all they talked about is when they were kids and their mom and dad ran the store. Milton handed his sister a flash-drive "it's from Moses" he told her "he said you'll know what to do with it. His sister who's name was Layla took the flash-drive "do you know what's on it" she asked Milton "no he just insisted that I give it to you" he replied "I'll take a look at it when I get back" she told him. Milton took a sip of his coffee "he also told me to tell you not to forget to read the note attached to it" Milton informed her, Layla looked at the flash-drive and saw a fold up piece of paper taped to the bottom of the case the flash-drive was in. "How is Moses doing" she asked Milton "he looks good, he looks like he's still working construction" Milton replied. They sat there talking to each other until Layla had to go back to work "you should come over for dinner mom sure would love to see you" Milton told Layla as she made her way to the front door "I can't promise nothing you know how busy I am" she said to him as she pushed the front door open "take care" he told her as she left through the door "bye" she replied.

Moses woke up he had turned back into his normal self it had started to rain, he felt the warm rain-drops on his face so he went in the cave where it was dry. Moses found a empty cloth sack in the cave which he used as a blanket to cover himself, the night felt cool and Moses had no clothes to keep warm just this old sack. Moses laid down in the cave cuddled up next to a large rock with his head braced up against the rock and the cloth sack covering his body, that's where he slept for the rest of the night.

Layla had seen what was on the flash-drive and read the note, the note said -please get this as soon a possible to the President- so she gave it to the Health Minister and he put it on the President's desk. President Myers was overseas in Romania at a Planning Conference with the IMC and was due back in Janoesha Harbour tomorrow evening.

Stacey and Shelby headed back to Shelby's house, Stacey was worried that the army would still be at her building so she decided on staying at Shelby's for awhile. Shelby was cool with it she didn't mind the company, frankly she was getting bored living in the house alone, she thought about moving men in but Shelby is a very attractive lady and all she seems to get are men that only wanted her for sex or monetary gain, she had bad luck in finding a man that was husband material. Shelby parked her car in the garage, both her and Stacey went in the house through a door in the garage that brought them in the hallway next to the kitchen. They took their shoes off in the hallway and made their way to the living room "so did you find what your were looking for" Shelby asked Stacey as she sat in the couch "yeah I did" Stacey replied "when are you going to call him" Shelby inquired. Stacey plugged in her phone to its charger, she saw that the battery was getting low "I'll call him right after my phone's charged" she told Shelby. Just as Stacey sat down in the couch Shelby got up and went to the kitchen "ARE YOU HUNGRY" she asked Stacey from the kitchen "A LITTLE" Stacey replied. Shelby made a platter of turkey sandwiches with mayo and lettuce, she brought it out to the living room and placed it on the center-piece "all I've got to drink is Blue Toucan" she told Stacey. Stacey did really need a beer to settle her nerves "great I'll take one" she replied, Shelby went back to the kitchen and grabbed two bottles of beer out of the fridge, when she got back to the living room she handed one to Stacey and sat in the rocking-chair beside the couch. "What do you think is going to happen to the army when this all comes out" Shelby asked Stacey as she took a drink of her beer "I'm not too sure" Stacey replied as she started to eat her second sandwich. Shelby took the last sandwich off the platter and started eating it "if we can't get in contact with Frank maybe we should check Base Laysan out" Shelby suggested to Stacey, Stacey gave her a smile "no we don't have to do that I'll speak with him on the phone" she told Shelby. Shelby turned on the TV "lets see what's on" she said as she used the remote to surf through the channels "Channel 8 news at 10 comes on in five minutes" Stacey told her, Shelby switched the channel to channel 8 and waited to the news came on. She got up out of the rocking-chair and brought the empty platter to the kitchen, while Shelby was busy in the kitchen Stacey checked the charge on her phone, it wasn't quite fully charged yet so she plugged it back on the charger and sat back in the couch to watch the news. On the news they showed President Myers in his private jet coming home from a meeting with the IMC in Romania they were talking to him about the taxation of all minerals mined on Janoesha Harbour and how local miners are being over taxed on their products. President Myers stated that there will be a decrease in the Mineral Taxing Laws for local miners on Janoesha Harbour in the coming year. The news also showed what was currently happening at the Space Lab, it showed men wearing white jump-suits and mask sifting through the rubble for evidence. Janet Jacobson was reporting there live she stated that re-construction of the Transfer Wing will begin next month and for anyone that works at the Space Lab should meet with Lieutenant Gormann for proper clearance before they start back to work next month. "Who are those people in the jump-suits" Shelby asked Stacey "I don't know but they're not JBI" Stacey replied "what do you mean" Shelby inquired "well I don't see any fire-trucks there so their not fire-investigators and the JBI doesn't investigate local fires, it leads me to wonder who these people are" Stacey explained to Shelby "could they be the police" Shelby asked "no the police only showed up to help those who were injured along with the ambulance, after everyone was taken to the hospital their jobs were over" Stacey told her and continued "no this is something else, I believe the army brought in their own investigators to sustain this cover-up" she said to Shelby. "A cover-up eh" Shelby said with a intriguing look on her face "yep in order for them to be the JBI they would have to go through the president first and we both know that the army can't afford to do that" Stacey told her.

After speaking with Lieutenant Gormann Frank got back to his jeep and left the Space Lab, he headed back to Base Laysan. During his conversation with Gormann he turned off his cell-phone so he wouldn't be distracted, on the way home he turned it back on and saw that Karen called him once she left a message saying that she put away a plate of food for him in case he came back late. For Frank this was late, driving on Highway 32 at 10:15 at night wasn't something he usually did, the highway was practically empty at this time. The ocean took on a magical metallic animation as the moon's light reflected off of it, Frank could hear in the distance the horns of cruise-liners and the squawking of albatrosses as they swoop down in the water to catch fish. It didn't take Frank long to get back to the base as he pulled into the base he waved to the MP Officer at the front gate to let him in, the gate opened up and Frank drove in. Frank took his phone out of the cradle on the dash-board and put it in his shirt pocket just then his phone started ringing, the number on the call-display wasn't a number he seen before so he answered it "hello Staff Sergeant Frank Allister". It was Stacey Lane Moses girlfriend "hey Stacey how are you" he asked surprise to hear her voice, Stacey told him about the incident that happened at the Space Lab and what happened to Moses "where is Mo now" he asked her, she told Frank that he was somewhere in the Black Forest. Stacey asked Frank if there was any help for Moses "I don't know but I'm certainly going to find out" he replied. Frank pulled up in his driveway and put his jeep in park, he sat there speaking on the phone with Stacey "where is the flash-drive now" Frank asked her, Stacey told him that she didn't know "don't worry I'll find a cure" he assured her "okay goodbye try to get some sleep" he told her before he hung up the phone. Frank got out of his jeep and went up to the front door of his house he took a key out of his pants pocket and unlocked the door. Slowly pushing the door open as he walked in trying his best not to wake anyone up he put his work-bag down on the floor next to a small night-table where he placed his car-keys. Frank sat on a chair in the living room thinking about what Stacey told him, so now he knows what they're hunting in the Black Forest 'if Moses has the flash-drive then he must of gave it to someone he could trust' Frank thought to himself "I need to find Moses" Frank said to himself.

Early the next day there was light rain falling down on the city of Tamerra, in Alan's Landing the rain had stopped and the sun was peeking through the clouds. At the Orange Gate the work day was just beginning the President's council members started showing up one by one to the President's chambers there was Walt Buyer the Defense Minister, Sue Onamagge Health Minister, Charles McFarlen Federal Energy Director, Jason Umaumbaeya Regional Commander for Merton Region and Erik Spencer Regional Commander for Passco Region. They all came in and sat around a large table waiting for the president to arrive, President Myers was due to show up earlier than scheduled, his private jet had landed at Crystal

International Airport 7:35am this morning but before heading to the Orange Gate he had to make a stop at home to collect some papers. President Myers got to the Orange Gate at 10am, he got escorted out of his limo by his security, they surrounded him as they walked him into the Orange Gate. The president went to his office and closed the door behind him, two men off his security stood guard outside his office. President Myers sat down behind his desk he felt good being back in Janoesha Harbour 'it was a long flight' he thought to himself, he then looked down on his desk and saw a flash-drive with a note stuck to it. He took the note and unfolded it, it was from Moses Uatobuu he recognized the name 'he rescued young Anna Levitroski a couple years back from her captor' the president thought to himself "I wonder what he wants" the president said to himself as he read the note. The note asked the president to view the flash-drive that it was important and based on national security so President Myers plugged the flash-drive into his laptop and started to watch its content.

Frank woke up early in the morning and made breakfast for himself Karen was still sleeping she had to go to the hospital in the middle of the night because of a work emergency. While eating breakfast Frank called into work letting them know that he couldn't make it in today due to a family emergency which wasn't true he was planning on heading out to the

Black Forest to find Moses. After he finished eating breakfast he went out to the shed in the backyard where he kept a selection of weapons, Frank wasn't too sure what to expected, from what Stacey told him on the phone he would need an arsenal. The shed was locked up with a large combination lock which Frank opened, inside the shed was a small stockpile of weapons, he had hand-grenades, machine-guns, hand-guns a whole load of ammunition there was also different types of fixation knives and Claymore mines. Frank grabbed a AR-15 machine-gun a few grenades and a fixation Bowie-knife that looked like a small sword. He carried them over to his jeep and loaded them in the trunk behind the back seats, he went back to the shed and grabbed two Claymore mines and some rope, he then closed the door to the shed and put the lock back on it. Frank loaded the rest of the stuff in his trunk and then closed it, the fixation Bowie knife came with a black sheath that he wore hooked onto his belt around his waste. Frank left a note for Karen on the kitchen counter explaining where he was going and what for, so when she wakes up she's not totally surprise that he left early. He got in his jeep started it up and left for the hour and a half trip out to the Black Forest, it's been almost two years since Frank's bin out there.

President Myers had finished watching what was on the flash-drive and was in total shock to see this sort of thing happening right under his nose, he never okayed any program like this 'what's going on here' he thought to himself. President Myers was also shocked to see General Banes on the flash-drive 'the army has no authority to okay something like this it would need to be brought to council and signed off by me' the president thought to himself. President Myers put the flash-drive in his desk drawer and turned off his laptop, he had a council meeting to attend. He got up from behind his desk and left his office, two men from his security escorted him to his chambers. When he got to his chambers the other rest of members were waiting for him, they stood up out of their seats when they saw the president enter the room, he sat in a chair at the head of the table just then the members took their seats. "Is there anything new the council wants to speak on" President Myers asked "yes the state of the drinking water in Pearles" Sue Onamagge replied. The president looked around the room and noticed that there was one council member missing, it was Greg Olson "does anyone know where Mr. Olson is" President Myers asked the council "no he didn't show up" Charles McFarlen replied. "Okay Sue in this meeting we'll keep focus on the water problem out in Pearles right after the meeting I want to see Walt Buyer and two of the RC Elect for Merton and Passco regions in my office" the president informed council, the three council members agreed to show.

President Myers gave the floor to Sue Onamagge the Health Minister "thank you sir, for the past two years there has been a population growth in caiman crocodiles south of the Black Forest region some of them are getting into the reservoir and laying their eggs, the enzymes from the egg shells gets mixed into the water and if drank can cause a severe fever and headaches, there has been two cases of someone dying from drinking the water we have sent a group of hydrologist up to Pearles to take a sample of the water, theirs and our concern is that it's going to leek into the Sambar Horn River, we want to stop it before it gets to that stage" Sue informed council.

Jessepi was heading back out to the Black Forest, he had gotten all what he needed from Greg Olson and was now on Highway 30 he would exit off of Highway 30 and onto Route 41 in south Umni to get to the Black Forest. Jessepi just got off the phone with Ray Gatlain, Ray told him if he needed anymore men that he could send some over, but Jessepi refused. This had become personal for him he wanted to kill this thing by himself for what it did to General Teal and his crew. Jessepi saw the turn off for Route 41 and took it, Route 41 was a two lane road in Umni it took you through plush green meadows and rolling hills with barns and farm animals. As soon as you got out of Umni heading west the road went through thick forest, there was signs posted on the side of the road telling motorists to beware of wild animals. Jessepi drove down the road not really paying attention to any signs all he could think about is killing Silverback for killing Kelso and Bruno. He had picked up some arrows with exploding tips and a bazooka, he wasn't going to leave Janoesha Harbour until this thing was dead, he was a little wary about killing a female though, how would that look for his tough-guy reputation 'I'm a large game hunter I don't murder women and children' Jessepi thought to himself as he took a half eating energy-bar out of his shirt pocket and started eating it. Plus that lady is a journalist for TJNX News her death would be televised all over Janoesha Harbour putting Jessepi in a bad position with the local authority and he was going to be nobody's patsy. 'If Greg Olson wanted that lady dead he would have to ask someone else to do it' Jessepi thought to himself. Jessepi was now entering the southeastern Black Forest region he took his hand-gun out of its holster and rested it on the dash of the humvee, he knew while being in the Black Forest that Silverback could attack at anytime so he was cautious of any movement up in the trees. Jessepi wasn't too far from where General Teal previously had a base set up, he knew that he was entering in the central Black Forest region and decided on taking a look around the base. About a half a mile east of highway 31 on Route 41 Jessepi turned off the road and started driving north through the woods he drove over decaying logs, small rocks and bushes doing his best not to crash into any trees but the rugged terrain and the humvee bouncing up and down proved this very difficult. It didn't take him too long to get to the mobile base, when he got there he saw the massive carnage of dead soldiers scattered all over the base. He got out of the humvee and walked around while holding his hand-gun he was looking for General Teal's body and any signs of where Silverback was. He never did find General Teal's body but he did find a piece of paper that struck his interest, Jessepi picked up the paper off the ground and unfolded it, it was a roughly sketched map of how to get to Crest Climb a part of the Turynfoymus Mountain Range. 'I wonder who this belongs to' Jessepi thought to himself 'maybe it was dropped by the beast' Jessepi smiled at that thought, he crumpled up the paper and tossed it away "could that be where he's heading to" Jessepi said to himself, the map indicated that it was in the western Black Forest region. Jessepi looked around and saw that there was nothing here for him and the whole reason he came here was to kill Silverback so he decided that he would head out to Crest Climb. Jessepi got back in the humvee and took out of the glove-compartment a road-map of the Black Forest as he studied the map he saw that Route 41 went north just east of Highway 31 but it stopped about four miles south of the Turynfoymus Mountain Range no roads went up to the mountain range only hiking trails. Jessepi folded back up the road-map and put it back in the glove-compartment, he started up the humvee and headed back to Route 41. He was going to get as close to the mountain range as possible and then hike from there, Jessepi was trying to figure out why Silverback would head to the mountains, what was his strategy, 'maybe it was the view-point' Jessepi thought to himself "if you're up high you're able to see over the trees and spot anything coming in" he said as he smiled to himself. Jessepi made a right turn onto Route 41 and headed east. When he got past Highway 31 he stopped the humvee and took a look at the road map again 'there must be a back way in' he thought to himself. On the map it showed that Route 5 came from the west and went north when it hit the Black Forest it went around the western section of the mountain range to its northwest end where it turns into a logging road that leads up into the mountain, this was the route Jessepi would take.

Greg Olson just arrived at the Orange Gate a few minutes after the council meeting ended, he was heading down the building's main hallway on the first floor to his office when he was stopped by the president's secretary. She informed him that he had an appointment with the president's board of council "what time is it for" he asked her "two pm don't be late" she replied "thank you" he said as he smiled at her. When Greg got to his office he opened the door and went in, he took off his suit-jacket and hung it on the back of the chair that was behind his desk, he sat down in the chair looking concerned about the board of council meeting he had to attend. He sat there wondering if the president found out about the Primate Program and if so has he connected him to it "that fucking journalist" he said under his breath. Greg decided on calling Ray Gatlain, the phone rang twice and Ray picked up "hello the Farm Doctor Gatlain speaking" Ray said "hi Ray it's Greg" "oh hi Greg how's everything" Ray asked "I think we mite have a problem I was called into a council meeting by the president" Greg told Ray "don't worry it's probably a unrelated matter" Ray said "you mite want to call Jessepi and tell him to get rid of that journalist" Greg told him "relax he will, nobody knows anything, you mite want to be careful in what you say over the phone the line maybe bugged" Ray informed him "don't worry this line is a secured line just get rid of that journalist" Greg told him and continued "do it before she goes to Public Announcement Corp" "what about Mr. Uatobuu" Ray asked. "Don't worry he's in a bad light right now his credibility is slowly diminishing" Greg assured him "I heard from Jessepi that a flash-drive was stolen with some sensitive information on it, did you guys get it back" Ray asked him "no this is why I want that journalist taking care of" Greg replied "what if Mr. Uatobuu has it and gave it to the authority" Ray implied "if he did it would be on my desk remember I'm the RC Elect for Edward region I oversee the police force in Edward region" Greg reminded him. "Okay I'll tell Jessepi" Ray said "thank you" Greg replied and hung up the phone, Greg wondered if there was a possibility that Moses could have friends here at the Orange Gate being that he's an ex-soldier in the Janoesian Army he's also well known in Janoesha Harbour for his heroics a couple years back in the rescue of little Anna Levitroski, the president also gave him a metal for that.

Stacey had woken up from sleeping on the couch, she sat up in the couch and stretched the sleep out of her body she then with her hand brushed her hair out of her face. There was dry tear tracks on her face from last night when she was on the phone with Frank, she had broke down crying on the phone pleading with Frank to help Moses. Frank was her only hope to find a cure for Moses, "good morning" she heard Shelby say from behind the couch "good morning" Stacey replied as she scratched her head. Shelby handed her some toiletries and a towel "there's extra toothbrushes and wash cloths in the washroom" Shelby told her "thank you" Stacey said to her as she went to the washroom to take a shower. Shelby went to the kitchen to prepare something to eat, she decided on having bacon and eggs with toasted English-muffins and a glass of orange juice. She made a plate for Stacey and left it on the kitchen counter with a cover on it so she had something to eat when she finished taking a shower. Shelby sat around the dining room table eating her breakfast 'I wonder what's on the agenda today' she thought to herself, she hadn't been to work in three days and wasn't too sure if she still had a job but for some reason this un-resting knowledge didn't effect her in anyway. She wondered if Stacey felt the same way, chances are the news room is probably on lock-down like the Space Lab plus nobody from work called her or left her a message asking how she was. Shelby finished eating her breakfast and brought the empty plate to the sink, she finished drinking her orange juice on the way there. She turned on the tap and rinsed the plate and glass and put them in the dishwasher that was beside the sink.

Frank took Highway 30 to Amaryllis Jaiz and then merged onto Highway 31, that's where he was right now heading north on Highway 31 to the Black Forest. From what Frank heard on base the army had setup a mobile base in the central Black Forest region so that's where he was heading. Frank had a friend that lived in Beryl Rado that he was planning on paying a visit, his friend worked for Black Forest Fishing & Game and knew the Black Forest in and out. Frank was going there to pick up a detailed map of the Black Forest plus his friend knew some scenic roads that aren't on the map. The closer he got to Beryl Rado the more raw rock formation he saw along the side of the road it almost looked like they had to blast through the rock to build the road. Frank could see a group of sambar deer in the bushes close to the road, he saw the sign for Beryl Rado saying 'Welcome to Beryl Rado Home of the Outdoors', the sign stated to turn right to get to the actual town so Frank made a right turn after the sign. The town was about a seven minute drive from the highway, Frank was now looking for his friend's place, he said he lived at the end of Granite Ridge Road just off the main strip. Frank drove down Beryl Rado's main road which was Route 2, Route 2 ran north to south, Frank headed north along Route 2 just after he pasted the local post office he spotted Granite Ridge Road on his left so he turned down the road and started looking for number 38. He found the house it was the fourth house in from the main road on the south-side of Granite Ridge Road. Frank parked his jeep on the road in front of the house, he got out of the jeep and went up to the front door and rang the doorbell. Thirty seconds later a large dark skinned man with dreads opened the door he was wearing blue-jeans and a tan khaki shirt "hey how you doing Serg" he asked Frank as he shook his hand "not too bad how are you Phil" Frank replied with a smile. "Come on in" Phil said with a smile as he invited Frank into his home, Phil escorted him to the dining room and they sat around the dining room table. "It's been around six months the last time I saw you" he said to Frank "yeah time sure flies doesn't it" Frank replied "can I get you anything to drink beer, juice" Phil asked Frank as he got up and headed to the kitchen "just a glass of water please" Frank replied. Phil came back with a glass of water for Frank and a can of Blue Toucan for himself, he opened the can of beer and took a drink "usually you come by my place for a reason so what's the reason today" Phil asked Frank "am I that predictable" Frank asked "yeah you are" Phil chuckled. Frank enjoyed sitting and talking with Phil but he needed to focus on what he came here for "well I'm here for a map of the Black Forest the ones the Rangers have" Frank told him "I see, tracking something are you" Phil asked him as he finished off his beer "you could say that" Frank replied "okay well give me a minute let me see if I can find one" Phil told him as he got up from around the table and headed to his bedroom. It wasn't long after that Phil came back out holding a map, he sat around the table and gave Frank the map "usually I charge for those maps but for you it's on the house" Phil told him "thank you" Frank said to him. Frank looked around and noticed that Phil's wife wasn't there and she was home all the time "where's Carly" Frank asked him "oh she went to the market, she should be back soon" Phil replied. Frank fold open the map and looked at it, it was so detailed it showed the mountain range and all the foot paths and logging roads, he smiled to himself Phil could see the approval on his face "is that what you were looking for" Phil asked him "yes" Frank replied as he folded back up the map "thank you again" Frank said to Phil as he shook his hand and they got up from around the table and went to the front door. "Heading out" Phil asked him "yeah I got to go" Frank replied "where are you heading" Phil inquired "the central Black Forest region" Frank replied "well just be careful there's been a few wild cat attacks in the region" Phil informed Frank as he walked with him to his jeep. Frank got behind the wheel, after he put the map on the front passenger seat he started up the jeep and drove off, as he drove away he looked through the rear-view mirror and saw Phil waving bye to him.

As Jessepi drove north on Route 41 he had his road map out on the front passenger seat, he would look at it every once in a while. He noticed that there was an old logging road that branched off from Route 41 heading west and met up with Route 5 so he decided that's the road he would take. Jessepi spotted the logging road on his left and turned onto it, the road wasn't paved it was a dirt road with grass growing down the middle of it. Jessepi was on the road for at lease five minutes when he seen the sign for Route 5, he made a right turn onto Route 5 and followed it all the way up into the mountains. Jessepi parked the humvee at the base of the mountain, grabbed his gear and started hiking to the top of the mountain.

Moses had woken up an hour ago he made a dress out of the cloth sack and went down the mountain to pick fruits so he would have something to eat. On his way back up the mountain he was eating a mango and holding a bunch of bananas, at the corner of his eye he saw a military humvee parked at the base of the mountain. He hid behind a tree nearby and watched, it looked like the humvee was empty but it was hard to tell 'if it was empty it would have had to gotten there somehow' he thought to himself then he remembered that he left his weapons in the cave. Moses started hiking back up the mountain to the top which would take a while, the top was 12,214 feet above ground level. As he made his way up the mountain he heard gun shots so he hid behind a rock, bullets whizzed over top of him and chipped into the rock he was behind. Moses tried his best not to turn into Silverback but he had nothing to defend himself so he felt threatened, he started transforming behind the rock "COME ON OUT DYING TIME IS HERE" he heard a voice call out. After the transformation Silverback jumped up on the rock and started beating his chest with his fist as he let out a roar, he then started running up the mountain whomever was shooting at him kept shooting at him as he made his way up the mountain. Silverback turned his head to see who it was, it was the same man that he fought in the forest, he had killed two of his men. Jessepi followed Silverback up the mountain but couldn't keep up with him so he set up camp half way up the mountain, there was a surfaced area surrounded by jagged rock where he put down his gear and sat planning a course of action. It didn't take Silverback long to get to the peak, when he got to the cave he collected his weapons and sat out in front of the cave waiting for Jessepi. He wondered how Jessepi found where he was and if there were more coming well at lease now he would be able to see them coming. Silverback sat there looking out at the Black Forest anticipating a platoon of soldiers, he was ready for any blitz attack they mite be coming with.

When Frank got to Route 2 he turned right and parked his jeep in front of a hardware store, he picked the map up off the seat, unfolded it and looked it over while he rest it on the steering-wheel. He saw on the map that Route 41 was the closest route to the central Black Forest region but he was facing the wrong direction so he made a U-turn and headed north. It didn't take him long to get to Route 41, when he got there he made a left turn onto it, Route 41 wasn't part of Beryl Rado it basically went through thick forest. Frank drove west along Route 41 he remembered on the map that he saw a beaten path that branched off of Route 41 and headed north and by the looks of it he was coming upon it pretty soon. He spotted the path and made a right turn onto it, the path was very rugged and unkept but it was nothing his 4x4 jeep couldn't handle. Frank drove on the path for about five minutes that's when he spotted the mobile base to his right through a cluster of trees, he parked his jeep on the path got out and headed to the base. When Frank got to the base he saw dead bodies of soldiers strewn all over the base along with smashed up vehicles, to Frank it looked like a bomb hit it. Frank called Phil on his cell-phone to send someone to clean the carnage up, Frank walked around looking for evidence of what happened he had one of his hands covering his nose the stench of decaying flesh was overbearing. He spotted a crumpled up piece of paper on the ground and picked it up, he opened it up and looked at it, it was a roughly sketched map of the Turynfoymus Mountains and how to get to Crest Climb its highest peak. Frank recognized the writing it was Moses so he folded it up and put it in his pants pocket 'that must be where he is' he thought to himself. He headed back to his jeep and left back to Route 41, when he got to Route 41 he made a right turn onto it, the map stated that Route 41 eventually bends and heads north. Frank had his road map opened up on the passenger seat, as he drove on Route 41 he glanced over at it, on the map he noticed a logging road that branched off of Route 41 and met up with Route 5. When he got to the logging road he turned onto it after that it didn't take him too long to get to Route 5, he turned right onto Route 5. Frank was thinking about what to say to Moses and if he was that creature like Stacey said he was would he recognize Frank "I wonder who else knows where he is" Frank said to himself as he swerved his jeep preventing from hitting a Roan antelope that was crossing the road. Route 5 took Frank around the western section of the Turynfoymus Mountains to a clearing at the base of the mountain. As Frank entered the clearing he saw a military humvee parked there, he parked his jeep nearby under an Acacia tree got out and went around back to the trunk. He opened the trunk and took out his AR-15 machine gun, Frank knew that Moses was no longer in the army so the humvee didn't belong to him and he didn't see Moses F-150 anywhere and that made him wary. So he decided to bring some defense with him as he hiked up the mountain, he closed back the trunk, he had a canteen full of water on one of the back seats which he grabbed there was a strap attached to it so he hung it around his neck and headed up the mountain.

THE TRUTH COMES OUT

It was going on 2pm and Greg Olson was heading to the board of council meeting, when he opened the door to the president's chamber and stepped in, the president was in there with three council members Walt Buyer, Jason Umaumbaeya and Erik Spencer. They were sitting around a board room table "good afternoon Mr. Olson" President Myers said to Greg "good afternoon sir" Greg replied as he bowed in respect before taking his seat. "I called this meeting because a flash-drive was left on my desk today in which I took a look at, it seems that the army started and is funding a program which I was unaware of"

President Myers said and continued "do you know anything about this Mr. Olson" he asked Greg. "No sir I don't" Greg replied now feeling a little agitated "well I looked into it further and was told by numerous people that saw you at Base Laysan with General Banes" the president told him and continued "can you explain that" he asked Greg "sir I am the RC Elect for Edward region and Base Laysan does fall in my jurisdiction, I was just visiting the base to see how things were there" Greg explained. "Any campaigning or visiting of Base Laysan must be approved by me and the president, you know that" Walt Buyer interjected, Greg knew now that he was in a corner that he possibly couldn't get out of so he didn't say anything he just waited to hear what the president would say. There was forty seconds of silence as President Myers thought it over "your reprimandation is that you will be stripped of the RC Elect position for eight months in which a thorough investigation will be done on this matter, during that time the RC Elect position will be given to the Vice Elect for Edward region" President Myers said and continued "get your story straight Mr. Olson because after the eight months are up you will be put before the Federal Review Board and remember after this meeting is closed you have some documents to sign" the president told him "yes sir" Greg replied as a look of shame came over his face, the other three council member turned their chairs so their backs faced him as a sign of disgrace.

The trail up the mountain was a rugged one paved with jagged rocks that were so sharp that if you slipped and fell on one of them they would surely cut you open, the rocks were dusted with dirt. The trail snaked all the way up to the top of the mountain, Frank didn't mind the hike he was use to it this is where he did his policeman's training. Frank took it a step at a time being careful not to slip and fall, he hoped that Moses hadn't turned into the creature yet that would make it easy for him to perhaps take him to where he can get some help. Not too far up the mountain Frank spotted a surface area where he could rest for five minutes, just then he heard gun shots and saw bullets ricocheting off rocks close to him 'is someone shooting at me' he thought to himself as he ran for cover and hid behind a large rock. The shots were coming from above him up the mountain "that couldn't be Moses" Frank said to himself, the shooting had stopped. Frank crouched down behind the rock thinking what to do, just then he saw a Latin looking man walking down the trail wearing a outback hat and a poncho he was holding a SAR 80 assault rifle looking around searching for something. 'Was this the person that was shooting at him' Frank thought "highly possible" he said under his breath, 'that's probably his humvee parked at the base of the mountain. Frank waited as the man walked by the rock he was hiding behind, as soon as the man got a distance past the rock Frank got back on the trail and continued up the mountain. Jessepi looked behind him because he heard shuffling that's when he seen Frank heading up the mountain so he turned around and gave chase. Jessepi starts shooting at Frank, Frank looks behind him and saw Jessepi coming up behind him that's when he turned around and returned fire, Jessepi hid behind a decaying tree trunk as bullets whizzed by his head "WHO ARE YOU" Frank called out to him "DON'T TAKE ANOTHER STEP UP THIS MOUNTAIN" Jessepi told him "SORRY I CAN'T DO THAT I HAVE A FRIEND THAT I'M LOOKING FOR" Frank said "IF IT'S THAT CREATURE THEN YOU'RE GOING TO DIE HERE TO" Jessepi told him. Frank then realized that this guy was here to kill Moses (that wasn't going to happen on Frank's watch) and now he was threatening Frank's life, Frank continued shooting his AR-15 taking chunks out of the tree trunk Jessepi was hiding behind. Frank held the machine gun in one hand and continued hiking up the mountain as he every once in a while looked behind him to see Jessepi's position. Jessepi kept low as he left the tree trunk and hid behind a large rock by this time Frank was out of his view so Jessepi got back on the trail and headed up the mountain. Frank looked behind him and didn't see

Jessepi, the hike to the top of the mountain took about forty-five minutes for Frank to achieve, the top of the mountain had a surfaced area that had a cave dug into the actual peak of the mountain. Frank looked around but didn't see anyone "I guess he's not here" he said to himself as he took a drink from his canteen right then he heard a loud roar and looked to where it was coming from, he saw a Silver Back gorilla jump off the peak of the mountain and land right in front of him. The ground shook when Silverback landed in front of Frank causing Frank to almost fall over but Frank kept his balance as he pointed his machine gun at Silverback not knowing for sure if it was Moses. To Frank the primate's face looked almost human-like then Silverback spoke "what are you doing here" he asked Frank "Mo is that you" Frank asked Silverback as he lowered his gun shock and amazed to see him in this state "yeah it's me, I asked you what are you doing here" Silverback replied, Moses voice was deep and amplified "Stacey told me what happened so I came here to help" Frank told him. Frank noticed that Moses was holding a shield and a Kukri sword he also had a leather whip around his neck "are you the cause of that carnage in the Black Forest" Frank asked him "they want to kill me or capture me so they can make a army of soldiers like me, it's either that or contain their secret by killing me" Silverback replied. "Stacey mentioned a flash-drive do you still have it"

Frank asked him "no I gave it to a friend that works at the Orange Gate to give to the president" Silverback replied, Frank knew that the army wasn't going to stop hunting Moses "we need to get out of here Mo" Frank told him. Just then Jessepi got to the top of the mountain and started shooting at them "time to die ape" he told Silverback as he unloaded gunfire on him, Silverback put his shield in front of him to protect him from the bullets. Jessepi was about to fire his bazooka when Frank threw a grenade at him, the grenade went off hurling Jessepi onto a large rock and knocking him out. One side of Jessepi's face and chest was burnt his nose and left ankle were broken, Frank went over to where he was laying on the rock he turned Jessepi over on his stomach and cuffed his hands behind his back with a pair of flex-cuffs that he had on him. Frank leaned Jessepi up against the rock "where are you taking him" Silverback asked Frank "to a jail cell on Base Laysan" Frank replied and continued "but I'm here to help you so I'm going nowhere just yet" Frank said as he sat Jessepi down on the ground with his back still leaned up against the rock.

Stacey and Shelby just got back to Shelby's house from going to the news station and they were now sitting out in the backyard. When they went to the news station they didn't go in the building they just sat in Shelby's car and watched all the soldiers standing guard around the station "this couldn't be all for me there must be more to this" Stacey said to Shelby as she watched soldiers go in and out of the news station, they sat there across the street for ten minutes before they decided on driving away. Now they were in Shelby's backyard sitting on lawn-chairs drinking juice and staring out at the Atlantic "do you think your friend Frank will be able to help Moses" Shelby asked Stacey "Frank is in the Janoesian Army he would have a better chance than anyone else" Stacey replied "plus he may have more detailed knowledge of what's going on" she added. Stacey was hoping that Frank would be able to help Moses or knows somebody that will, she was worried for Moses and wondered if Frank found him and if they were safe, she took a drink of her juice and added more in her glass from the plastic jug that was on the small wooden table in between them. "You going to the Harbour Fair this year" Shelby asked her as she changed the subject to something positive "me and Moses was planning to" Stacey replied. Shelby could see that Stacey's mind was consumed with thoughts of Moses so she gave her five minutes by herself and got up and headed back in the house "I got some stuff to do inside but there's no rush take your time and enjoy the juice" she told Stacey as she left.

"So are you ready to go" Frank asked Silverback, Silverback thought about it for a minute "no I think

I'll stay" he replied "why would you want to do that" Frank asked him "I'm going to keep this change in me so I can put a stop to the military's corruption" Silverback told him "you can do that as your normal self" Frank said "I believe the citizens of Janoesha Harbour need a protector" Silverback replied. Frank thought that was really noble of Moses "are you sure about this" he asked Moses "I am" Silverback replied "okay I guess I'll be on my way, don't forget if you need anything I'm here for you" Frank told him, Frank looked over at Jessepi, Jessepi was just waking up from being knocked out, he went over to where Jessepi was and stood him up and escorted him down the mountain. Silverback sat there in front of the cave looking out at the Black Forest "I'll be home soon Stacey" he said to himself, he really loved Janoesha Harbour with all his heart and with these newly found powers of his he will protect it's citizens from crime and corruption.

General Banes was now in the Neural Testing wing of the hospital on Base Laysan, he was wearing a white robe and had his head bandaged. He was in a room with a neural psychiatrist that was showing him picture-cards and he had to say what the picture was. He was to be in that wing for nine days on the ninth day the doctors would check for any improvements, if he has improved he would get to go home if not he would stay for another nine days. The doctors told his wife that if he was able to go home that he couldn't go back to work for a couple months, they also prescribed him some medication (Tricyclic) and gave it to his wife to keep at home, they also gave her some painkillers for him. The doctors had him on Tricyclic and painkillers in the hospital he was taking them twice a day, he still couldn't move his mouth to talk the wounds hadn't fully healed so if he wanted to ask a staff member for something he had to write it on a piece of paper. General Banes ribs were also bandaged and a nurse had to push him around in a wheel-chair, he still had a lot of physical healing to go through.

Greg Olson was at home in his office sitting behind his desk watching a news coverage about the scandal on Base Laysan. They mentioned his name and how he was using tax payer's money to fund genial cloning without the approval of the federal government. Greg sat there staring at his flat-screen TV that was mounted on the wall occasionally filling a glass with Boukman Botanical Rhum that he bought at the liquor store. He finished the glass in two gulps and poured another, his eyes were filled with tears as he realized that his career and life was over not to mention his reputation, he could never show his face in public again. His phone was ringing but he just ignored it he had plans after finishing this forty ounce bottle of rhum in which he was almost done with. Greg took out of his desk drawer a black revolver and rested it on his lap, he poured the remainder of the rhum in his glass and downed it in one gulp he then picked up the revolver and put the barrel in his mouth, cocked back the hammer and pulled the trigger. The back of Greg's head splashed out on the wall behind him, Greg's body slumped over in the chair dead and the revolver fell out of his hand on the floor beside him.

It didn't take Frank long to get back to Base Laysan, with Jessepi handcuffed in the back seat of his jeep he was planning on dropping him off at the jail on base but first he was going to call Stacey to let her know that Moses was okay. Frank parked his jeep beside a variety store on base and dialed Stacey's number on his cell-phone, the phone rang twice and Stacey answered "hello" she said "hi Stacey it's Frank" he replied "oh hi Frank" she said glad to hear from him "so did you hear from Moses" she asked him "yeah he's out in the Turynfoymus Mountains" Frank replied "were you able to get him some help" she inquired "well about that, he said he doesn't want any help" Frank answered not sure how she would take it "what do you mean" she asked him with a concerned tone in her voice "I think it's better for you to talk with him in person" Frank said "he's at Crest Climb, you follow Route 5 into the mountains north of Tamerra" Frank told her "okay thanks Frank" she said and hung up. "Ain't love grand" Jessepi said sarcastically in the back seat referring to Stacey "Shut up I don't want to hear anything from you, you should be concerned about how many years you're going to be spending in prison" Frank told him, Jessepi smiled blankly at Frank. Frank started up the jeep and headed to the jail which was only a seven minute drive from where he was, Jessepi's phone started ringing which Frank had took from him and put on the dashboard of his jeep. "Is that your phone ringing" Frank said to Jessepi and picked it up off the dash "hello" Frank answered, it was a man's voice on the other end "who's this" the voice asked "this is Staff Sergeant Frank Allister of the Janoesian Army" Frank replied "who's this" Frank asked "this is Doctor Ray Gatlain, may I speak with Jessepi" Ray replied "sorry he's being brought to jail" Frank told Ray "under what charge" Ray asked Frank "weapon offenses and espionage to begin with" Frank replied "that's preposterous" Ray told him "if you want to talk with him you can after he's been booked in the jail" Frank told Ray then hung up the phone and tossed it back on the dash. "you can't hold me for too long" Jessepi told Frank "we'll see about that" Frank replied, Frank looked through Jessepi's wallet that he took from him as he pulled up to the jailhouse "so you're from Cuba" Frank said "what are you doing here" Frank asked him "deer hunting" Jessepi replied "you must be hunting pretty aggressive deer with that assault rifle" Frank said sarcastically. Frank parked his jeep in front of the jailhouse and got out he opened the back door "lets go time to get out" Frank said, Jessepi got out, Frank slammed the door shut and escorted Jessepi into the jailhouse. When Frank got to the front door of the jailhouse he had to be buzzed in by one of the guards on shift, as he stepped into the jailhouse with Jessepi there was a desk to his immediate left, behind it sat a MP officer "bringing one in for booking" Frank told the MP officer "prisoner's name" the officer asked Frank, Frank looked at Jessepi's ID in his wallet "Jessepi Montoya" Frank replied "date of birth" the officer inquired "August 7th 1981" Frank answered. The officer pointed down the hall "go to the room at the end of the hall to take his picture" he told Frank "thank you" Frank said to him and headed down the hall with Jessepi.

A channel eight news van from TJNX news was parked on the street in front of the Orange Gate, Janet Jacobson was reporting the latest news relating to the Space Lab, "hi this is Janet Jacobson reporting live from the Orange Gate, sources say that a flash-drive was sent to the president's desk, on the flash-drive revealed a secret program between the RC Elect of Edward region and General Terrance Banes a high ranking general in the Janoesian Army endorsing government funds to start up what they call the Primate Program, the program was started by a sub-section of the Janoesian Army to create stronger soldiers. Greg Olson RC Elect for Edward region was just stripped of his position and is now under internal review, General Banes is currently at the hospital on Base Laysan once he's released he will be charged in a military court for going outside his code of conduct and federal embezzlement" Janet Jacobson said. As she held the microphone in one hand she pointed with her other hand at the Orange Gate "right now inside the Orange Gate the president is speaking with Defense Minister Walt Buyer about money being siphoned out of military funds into an overseas account" Janet informed the public.

Stacey and Shelby was inside watching the news "I'm going to need to borrow your car tomorrow" Stacey said to Shelby "okay may I ask why" Shelby asked her "I'm going to see Moses, Frank told me where he is" Stacey replied "that's great we should both go" Shelby said "no this I have to do alone" Stacey told her. Once the news was finished Shelby switched off the TV "make sure you bring lots of water with you, the weather is suppose to be really hot tomorrow" she told Stacey "it's good that the general is going to be charged" Stacey said referring to what she heard on the news as she did her best to change the subject. Shelby smiled to herself as she realized that Stacey didn't want to talk anymore about Moses "yeah they're probably going to strip him of some of his metals" she said to Stacey "can they do that"

Stacey asked curiously "I'm sure if he's found guilty they can" Shelby replied. "They didn't say too much about the Space Lab and if it's under investigation for breaching it's company's mission statement" Stacey implied "there's definately going to be a lot of law-suits the courts are going to be packed this summer" Shelby said. Shelby got up out of the sofa and went to the kitchen to wash some dirty dishes that was left in the sink, Stacey was happy to see that the truth about the Space Lab was coming out in the media.

Ray Gatlain was finishing up some paperwork in his office, he was thinking about Jessepi ever since he got off the phone with Frank. He couldn't afford to have Jessepi sitting in jail, he is one of his best hunters and also he's been pulling in monetary gain for The Farm from he started working here, he would need to see what he can do to get him released and brought back to Cuba even if he has to pull some strings. Ray knew someone that worked for the immigration service on Janoesha Harbour this person owed Ray a favour that has been fifteen years past due 'maybe this is the time to cash in' Ray thought to himself. He shuffled up some paper on his desk and put them in a paper-folder, smiling to himself while approving in his head his ingenius plan to get Jessepi out of jail.

General Banes was in the solarium that was on the fifth floor of the hospital, he was sitting in his wheel-chair looking out through a large display window at the neatly trimmed grass below decorated with Breaded Wind Chimes hedging around its perimeter and a couple green buttonwood trees on its property around their trunks grew flowers of all different colors. General Banes just sat there staring out into the open world, down the hall from the solarium was a large booth occupied by two nurses and a security-guard just coming upon that room were a group of men one of them was Federal Defense Minister Walt Buyer and to the right of him were three (MP) Military Police Officers an to the right of them were two JBI Agents. One of the MP offiicers knocked on the door of the booth, the security-guard opened the door "hi can I help you" he asked "here to see patient Terrance Banes" the MP told him, one of the nurse checked on the computer for Terrance Banes and found him "he was just brought to the solarium it's down the hall and to your left" she told the officer, the security-guard buzzed the group of men in. Walt Buyer was holding a federal warrant rolled up in his hand that he was going to serve to General Banes, the men headed down the hall to the solarium, when they got there they opened its sliding-door and went in General Banes was still there staring out the window. The men walked over to the general and stood around him, the general didn't move from his position, Walt Buyer unrolled the warrant and read it in front of General Banes "Terrance Banes

I'm here to serve you this federal warrant for your arrest and for a search of your house and whatever other property you might have" Walt read and then placed the warrant on General Banes lap "these men are here to take you to the jail an in two days you will be transferred to Greystone" Walt informed the general. General Banes didn't respond to any of this he just sat there staring out through the window as if he were parylized in a tranquil bliss, one of the MP officers took a hold of his wheel-chair and wheeled him out of the room, the JBI agents made sure that he was handcuffed to the wheel-chair as they took him down the hall.

After Jessepi got his pictures taken Frank escorted him to his jail-cell "welcome to your new home for a couple of days" he told Jessepi and shoved him in the cell right after he took his handcuffs off, the cell's door slammed shut "you're making a big mistake" Jessepi said to Frank "in a couple days you'll be transferred to Greystone where you'll be living for a long time" Frank told Jessepi as he headed back to the front door to get buzzed out. As Frank exited the jailhouse and got back to his jeep he was thinking about Moses and Stacey, would it ever be the same for them he knew they really loved each other 'maybe something good will come out of this' he thought to himself as he climbed back in his jeep and started it up. He backed out of his parking spot and entered onto the road, he was planning on stopping off at the coffee shop for a muffin and a coffee.

A new day opened up on Janoesha Harbour with partially cloudy skies, Stacey was packing a cooler with drinking-water and snacks for her road trip out to the Turynfoymus Mountains. She loaded the cooler in the trunk of Shelby's grey 2012 Pontiac Sunfire, Shelby stood outside the front door to her house watching as Stacey got ready for her trip "remember to put some gas in the tank, there's not enough to carry into the mountains" she told Stacey. Stacey closed the trunk and got behind the wheel, she stuck the key inn the ignition and started the car up its engine sound very good like it was well maintained and taken care of, the car rolled slowly down the driveway, as Stacey adjusted the rear-view mirror she saw Shelby waving bye to her so she stuck her hand out the driver's side window and waved back. Stacey was going to take Highway 32 north to the Route 5 exit, as soon as she got out of Shelby's neighborhood she merged onto Highway 32. Stacey was thinking of what to say to Moses when she got there, she really wanted to apologize to him for all he had gone through, she was the cause of them turning him into this creature "I'm sorry Mo" Stacey said to herself. It was a fifteen minute drive to the Route 5 exit, Stacey exited onto Route 5 that took her into the northwest section of the Turynfoymus mountain range. When she entered into the Black Forest Route 5 turned into a two lane dirt road, Stacey was handling the car pretty good for being out of practice, she did have her driver's license just no car and this was the first time in a long time that she was behind the wheel. She was doing good going over bumps carefully and shifting gears when she's suppose to (and believe me there was a lot of bumps), she drove by a sign that stated that there was wildcats in the area but didn't notice it and had to slam on the brakes to avoid from hitting a family of Oncillas that were crossing the road. The car came to a screaching stop just a foot away from the group of cats "christ" Stacey said rubbing her head as she took a deep breath of relief knowing that she didn't hit anything, she sat there trying to calm her nerves down she was a little excited about seeing Moses and needed to pay attention in what she was doing. She took a couple deep breaths and a drink of water and continued driving, she should know better that the Black Forest is nowhere to speed. Route 5 took her around the western section of the Turynfoymus mountains to a clearing at the base of the mountain, she spotted a hiking path that snaked up into the mountain, at the foot of the path was a wooden sign the read 'Crest Climb' "this must be it" Stacey said to herself, she parked the car under an Acacia tree that was nearby.

Gwen Stevens took the Inner Hoop to Alan's Landing she got off at the Bowling Dice Lane stop where most of the corporate office buildings were, Bowling Dice Lane is a main street in downtown Alan's Landing that runs east west most of the street has different types of office buildings like government, banking & investment, legal firms and corporate. Gwen had come to Alan's Landing for a job interview, she still hasn't heard back from the Space Lab about going back to work and she couldn't wait any longer so she did some online job searching and found a company in Alan's Landing that's looking for a pathologist. Gwen left the Inner Hoop station and stepped out into the busy streets of Alan's Landing, she stood at the corner of Shore Street & Bowling Dice Lane waiting for traffic on Bowling Dice Lane to go by so she could cross the street but she gave up on that and used the crosswalk like she saw a group of people doing. Gwen headed east on Bowling Dice Lane, she was twenty minutes early so she decided that the first coffee shop that she sees she going to go in, and just then she spotted one on her side of the street 'Perks N Roast' was its name, Gwen opened its front door and went in. Inside the coffee shop was quite spacious, from the front door to your immediate left was the front counter behind the counter a young cashier stood behind her was a large menu of different types of coffees and teas that they brew there, you can even order sandwiches and pastry. To the right of the front counter is a group of fancy round tables with four chairs around each of them, Gwen took a seat at one of the tables and waited for a server to come by. While waiting she practiced what she would say when she met the employer today, Gwen was a little nervous about the interview (she had butterflies in her stomach) if the employer would like her enough to consider her for the position, a server came to her table "what can I get you mam" the server ask her, Gwen looked over at the menu behind the front counter "can I get a large Blue Mountain roast and a couple cherry puff pastry" Gwen replied "yes mam I'll be right back with that" the server told her and left to start her order.

'The shade from the tree will keep the engine cool so it doesn't over heat' she thought to herself as she got out and slammed the car door shut behind her, she went and opened the trunk and took out two bottles of water from the cooler that was inside. Stacey put on her head a straw-hat with a wide brim and she had sunglasses on, she also made sure to wear hiking-boots, the track-shorts she was wearing were a little revealing though but they left some to the imagination. Stacey closed the trunk and headed for the trail that lead up into the mountains, as she began hiking the trail she could hear vehicles in the distance she ignored the sounds and just figured that it was sound being carried from the highway. The incline up hill made this hike feel like a workout to Stacey 'maybe I should of grabbed an extra bottle of water' she thought to herself as she took a drink of water.

The server came back with Gwen's order and placed it on the table in front of her "enjoy mam if you need anything I'm over by the counter" the server told her "thank you" Gwen said to the server, the server left to check on another table. There was cream and sugar already on the table they were next to a box of stir-sticks, Gwen poured some cream in her coffee and also emptied out a packet of cane-sugar into it she took a stir-stick and stirred her coffee for a bit. While stirring the coffee she munched on the puff pastry until they were gone, she sat there sipping on her coffee and looking at her cover-letter seeing if there was any corrections to be made on it. After she finished her coffee she got up from around the table and went over to the front counter to pay her bill which she did on her debit-card, she left the coffee shop and continued east along Bowling Dice Lane. The place she was looking for was named Med Lab and by the directions she was given it was close by, Gwen hadn't walked too far from the coffee shop when she spotted the company Med Lab on her right, she looked at the large blue sign over the front door of the company and took a deep breath as she straightened up her dress and fixed her hair, she walked up the steps to the front door and opened it.

A sweeper-team of the Janoesian Army was deployed on the central Black Forest region along with a clean-up crew. The sweeper-team was led by Lieutenant Gormann and was ordered by Walt Buyer by request of the president, President Myers sent the sweeper-team into the Black Forest to find and capture whatever animal or thing destroyed the Space Lab and killed a platoon of soldiers, he heard from witnesses that it was an ape-like creature. The clean-up crew was a ten men Body Clean-up Crew & Sanitation ordered by Sue Onamagge also by request of the president, the crew's job was to bag and despose of all the dead bodies within the central Black Forest region. After the body clean-up sanitation trucks would come in and spray a clear organic liquid that contained nitrogen, phosphorus and potassium on all the trees and plant life washing off whatever blood and grime is on them. Sue Onamagge insisted on this being that the Black Forest is a big part of Janoesha Harbour's tourism and it should look presentable an free from any life threatening bacteria also the Starr Points Chalet is located in the central Black Forest region. The clean-up crew setup a grid-pattern and spent the whole day combing through the central Black Forest region bagging bodies and loading them onto flat-bed trucks. The sweeper-team patroled through the Black Forest looking for the creature everyone was talking about but still didn't find anything "sir do you think this thing is still out here" a Corporal Bennet asked Lieutenant Gormann as he helped some soldiers setup base-camp "if it is we'll find it" Gormann replied. Gormann kept in contact with his men by CB-radio, checking in with them every ten minutes, he made sure Bennet also had a radio, his men formulated a military grid pattern as their search procedure as they patroled the forest.

Walt Buyer was in his office at the Orange Gate going over some paperwork when his phone rang, he picked it up "hello Walt Buyer speaking" he answered "hi Walt" the voice said, it was the president "hi Mr. President" Walt replied "how's everything at the Black Forest" the president asked him "they haven't found anything yet sir" he replied "let them know not to be loud in their search remember the Starr Point's is filled with tourist we don't want to raise any concerns" President Myers told him "yes sir" Walt replied. "I also have some bad news" the president said and continued "they found Greg Olson in his house dead from a gunshot wound, apparently his wife came home after shopping and found him in his office sitting behind his desk dead" President Myers told Walt "oh my God that's awful" Walt said "do they know what happened" Walt asked the president "the JBI just showed up at the scene and

(CSA) Crime Scene Analysis are studying the crime scene" the president replied "I was told by a person there that it looks like suicide" the president told Walt "wow! That's sad is his wife okay" Walt inquired "yes she was brought to Tamerra Memorial Hospital they say she fainted when she saw her husband and EMS revived her before bringing her to the hospital to get checked out" President Myers informed Walt. The contracts that Greg signed to sit before the Federal Review Board will be striked off as null and void by the president and later on today at Jordan Square the Vice Elect for Edward Region Genesee Lockport will be sworing in as Regional Commander for Edward Region. "I have to inform Genesee about this" President Myers told Walt "how do you think she's going to take it" Walt asked him "I'm not too sure, anyway it's a new position for her" the president replied "yes she'll be happy to hear that" Walt said. President Myers hung up the phone on his end so Walt hung up his phone, Walt couldn't believe that Greg Olson took his own life it goes to show that corruption doesn't pay especially for a public figure like Greg was, when it comes down to it all he had was his reputation and when that was tainted and destroyed what else did he have, his wife was going to find out about his crimes and he couldn't live with that. Walt shook his head in unbelief and got back to his paperwork.

It took Stacey just under an hour to hike up to the top of the mountain, from the top she could see out over the Black Forest, those vehicles that she heard earlier were military trucks she could see the tops of them driving through the Black Forest. When Stacey got to the top of the mountain she looked around for Moses and spotted him sleeping in a cave, he had turned back into his normal self, she went over to the cave to get a good look at him that's when he rolled over and sat up he yawned and stretched the sleep out of his body. "Moses" she said to him, he looked at her "you're here" he said "I am" she smiled at him, he was naked so he wrapped a towel around himself and crawled out of the cave, stood up and hug her "I missed you so much Stacey" he told her "yes I know I missed you to that's why I'm here we need to get you some help" she told him. Moses knew that Stacey was only trying to help that's what he loved about her she wasn't selfish she thought of her friends first before herself "I've decided on keeping this creature I turn into" Moses told her "why Mo, if you do you'll always be hunted by them" she replied shocked to hear that from him "I'm always on the side of good they can't change how I feel inside" Moses said while holding Stacey's hands. "What about us" Stacey asked him "I'll never leave you Stacey I'll always be here close to you" he replied, she kissed him on the cheek "I know you will" she said to him and continued "but I thought you wanted to get married and start a family" she asked him "we still can do that love" he replied "not if you're that creature" she said to him. Moses looked into her eyes those eyes that captured his heart three years back "there is so much corruption and injustice in the military and parts of government here that no one could do anything about, now that I have the ability to put a stop to it you want me to give it up" he said to Stacey "I just want you to think about the people that are close to you and how you'll be effecting their lives" she told him. They could hear the rumbling of the trucks motors even louder now as if they were closer "we need to leave before they find out that we're up here" Stacey told Moses "don't worry we're safe" Moses assured her, Moses held one of Stacey's hands over her head and twirled her around, inspecting her civilian wardrobe "nice shorts" he told as he looked at her butt-cheeks peeking out from behind her shorts and this inspired him to lightly squeeze her ass, she let out a giggle and they hugged again "I wore them for you" she told him. "Did you bring any clothes for me" he asked Stacey "no but I think there's a pair of overalls in the trunk of the car" she replied, Stacey was afraid for Moses she didn't want him to get hurt "how are you as one going to stand up to the entire Janoesian Army" she asked him "have a little faith in me honey" he replied "I just don't want you to get hurt" she told him and continued "so now you're the protector of Janoesha Harbour, that's alot to put on your plate" she said sarcastically "the country needs this type of balance" he told her. Stacey looked at Moses and knew he believed in what he was saying and that there was no way she could change him from thinking that way a noble hero the protector of his fellow citizens, but all heros have a name "what should they call you" Stacey asked him, Moses smiled at her "Silverback" he replied.

The phone rang at the jailhouse on Base Laysan one of the MP's on duty answered it, it was a long distant call from Cuba "Ollie Jail Base Laysan" the officer said "hi this is Debra Martinez the Secretary of the Executive Committee here in Cuba I was informed that you have a Jessepi Montoya there" the voice on the other end said "yes we do he's to be transferred to federal prison in two days after he sees the Justice Of Peace" the officer told Debra "and where will he be seeing the Justice Of Peace" Debra asked him "at the courthouse in Alan's Landing, that where they will set the amount for bail" the officer replied "who am I speaking to" Debra inquired "Corporal George Anders" the officer replied "well Corporal Anders I shall be in Alan's Landing in two days to speak with your Justice Of Peace" Debra informed George. Corporal Anders was sitting in a office booth facing the jail cells, he looked over at

Jessepi in his cell staring back at him, Jessepi smiled at him "yes mam" Corporal Anders replied and hung up the phone. "Is something wrong officer" Jessepi asked George because he could see a look of concern on his face "be quiet prisoner and go to sleep" George told Jessepi "who just called there" Jessepi inquired "if you don't be quiet I'm going to come in there and put you out" George warned him. Jessepi nodded his head and smiled to himself "yes I see" Jessepi said as he sat down on the bed in the cell "someone called about me" he said to George "it won't be long now till I'm back in Cuba" Jessepi told George "you're not going anywhere prisoner" George told him. "I heard you mentioning the Justice Of Peace, is that who determines the amount for bail" he asked George "if you don't SHUT UP I'm going to crack you over the head" George told him, Jessepi laid down in bed looking up at the ceiling with his hands behind his head thinking about Cuba and the Farm and how he's going to plan his next attack on that ape. He knew that Doctor Gatlain was working on his release from jail and soon as he got released he would get reinforcements, enough fire-power to kill that creature, Jessepi smiled at his thought 'only two nights' he thought to himself he closed his eyes and got some sleep.

THE END

Printed in the United States
By Bookmasters